SINCLAIR TERRITORY

by

JANE CORRIE

Harlequin Books

TORONTO • LONDON • NEW YORK • AMSTERDAM • SYDNEY • WINNIPEG

Original hardcover edition published in 1976
by Mills & Boon Limited

ISBN 0-373-02038-4

Harlequin edition published January 1977

Printed in Canada

CHAPTER ONE

DELIA COURTENAY hoped the transport her Aunt Lucy had promised would not be too long in arriving. The small airless office she sat in was making her drowsy. She twisted the two rings on her third finger, and dropped her hands apart with an impatient movement; it was a habit she was getting into and one she must cure herself of. Her glance rested on her luggage, and she wondered how she would take to the new life, but she had to do something. She fervently hoped her aunt would not want to go into everything when she heard about the marriage.

Even after nine months Delia found it hard to talk about. It wasn't that she wanted to forget, it was just that time had not yet healed the wound, and she doubted it ever would. Fate had given her only three weeks of blissful happiness before snatching Philip away. Her life had begun and ended in that brief space of time. She had waved him good-bye on that fateful journey, his first business trip after the honeymoon, and the plane had crashed over the Alps.

As Delia stared out at the bare dry ground of the landing run, she wished she had written and told her aunt of her marriage and subsequent widowhood, but it had all happened so quickly. Philip's whirlwind courtship, the marriage, in spite of bitter opposition from his sister and aunt, who were convinced Delia was a fortune-hunter.

At thirty-five, Philip had been considered a confirmed bachelor, thus it was something of a shock when he entered into a determined pursuit of Delia, his new secretary. A shock all round, as Delia had not considered herself of a disposition to arouse such interest from a man of Philip's standing, for Delia was not a beauty and would have termed herself as 'pass-able' had her opinion been sought.

She was small, with elfin-like features and red-gold hair, and her large cornflower blue eyes were, she felt, her only claim to beauty. She was shy, and no match for Philip's relations, who had not only claimed the estate after his death, but had done their level best to snatch back the property he had bought for himself and Delia to live in after their marriage.

Delia had one ally – Philip's cousin John. John was a solicitor, and but for his efforts on her behalf she would not have been able to afford to make this trip half-way across the world to join her aunt, her father's sister. Aunt Lucy had more or less demanded her presence. Now that Delia's father had died, there were no other living relatives, and as her aunt had put it in her forthright way, 'There's just me and you, girl, and I'm not getting any younger, so you book that passage!'

Her aunt had wanted to pay Delia's fare, but Delia would not hear of it. The family had an ordinary b ck-ground, what money there was had to be earned the hard way. Delia knew Aunt Lucy had worked for what she had got, indeed was still working, running a ho tel for girls employed in the canning factories in the small township of Sinclair, in the Murrumbidgee Irrigation Area, New South Wales.

Glancing at her watch, Delia saw it was five-thirty. Wiping the moisture away from her forehead, she stared up at the fan whirling monotonously above her, and wondered whether it was working. The young pilot who had brought her from Sydney had offered to make her a drink, but Delia had refused, knowing he was behind schedule and wanted to get on.

Aunt Lucy had warned Delia that it might be a while before she was collected as it depended on someone being available to drive the van. It was, she said, the busy season.

Delia sighed and went back to her musings. She had not written and told her aunt of the marriage simply because Philip had come up with the wonderful idea of a visit to her that summer. Delia's eyes moistened as she heard his voice again. 'We'll just walk in, darling, and bring her back with us, if she wants to come back, that is. In any case, she ought to be thinking about retiring now, surely? Anyway, we'll see.'

The trouble was neither Delia nor her aunt were good correspondents, and often months went by without communication. Christmas cards and birthdays, of course, were acknowledged, but once Aunt Lucy had made known her wish that Delia should join her it was left to Delia to make the next move.

It had taken Delia a long time to get back on to terms with life after Philip's death. Somehow it seemed pointless to write then. She would tell her aunt when she met her. Quietly, and she hoped, unemotionally.

Seeing a dust cloud in the distance, Delia watched as it neared the airfield. Minutes later a blue van pulled up outside the building. Picking up a case, Delia went to the door.

A thin wiry man with a slouch hat and nut brown face grinned at her. 'Howdy! Miss Dene?'

Delia saw no point in correcting him; they would all know soon enough she was Mrs. Courtenay. She smiled back at him and nodded. He collected her luggage and placed it in the back of the van, then opened the passenger door for her. Delia climbed in.

Starting the engine, the man gave her a quick look and another grin. 'Lucy's sure tickled pink you made it after all,' he commented. 'Ain't talked of nothing else for days. Er – Paddy's the name,' he supplied helpfully.

'How do you do, Paddy?' Delia replied politely. 'Do you work at the hostel?'

His grin grew wider. 'Kinda like Lucy to hear that,' he said. 'No, ma'am. I'm from the farm. We kinda help out like, now and again.'

'Oh, you're a farmer, are you?' Delia asked.

This produced another grin. Pushing his hat back, he answered, 'Well, no, ma'am, I'm like one of the hands.'

'Oh,' said Delia. 'Sort of stockman, are you?'

He chuckled. 'Guess you've got the wrong kind of farm. Fruit farming, I meant.'

'Oh,' she said a second time, then subsided; canning factories would have to have fruit, wouldn't they? Aunt Lucy hadn't said much about the district, or come to that, anything but the hostel. Delia felt she had a lot to learn.

They were now passing a sparsely built up area. This must be the town, she thought. Delia knew it was not a large one by English standards, and remembered Aunt

Lucy telling her during her last visit home five years ago that it was more in the nature of a large village. There were the factories, of course, one each side of the town, and several stores and offices.

Gazing out, Delia noticed the name Sinclair cropping up with monotonous regularity, and she wondered why tradesmen had adopted the town's name rather than their own.

As they passed through what appeared to be the main street, her companion spoke again. 'Soon be there,' he commented. 'Perhaps now you're here you can get Lucy to ease up a bit. No use us telling her. She might listen to you,' he said slowly as he negotiated a bend.

Delia looked at him. 'Is Aunt Lucy ill?' she asked.

'Well, it's nothing serious as yet,' he answered hastily, aware of the concern in Delia's voice. 'She's had an ulcer for years and mighty touchy about anyone knowing, hates the idea of giving up. Don't tell her I told you,' he added quickly. 'She'd bawl me out for what she'd say ain't none of my business, but she needs a rest. She ain't so young as she was.'

Delia digested this news and was glad she had come. One would certainly see Aunt Lucy got the rest she needed. She cast a quick glance at Paddy now concentrating on his driving and felt warmed to him. He was no youngster himself. Delia wondered whether he was a bachelor and interested in Aunt Lucy, then quickly smothered a grin as she imagined her aunt's reaction to this thought; Aunt Lucy was a born spinster and proud of the fact.

The van slowed down and pulled up in front of a

large sprawling building. Delia got out and gazed at it. It was three storeys high and might almost be put in the preservation class! She wondered how old it was.

Collecting her cases, Paddy led the way up the short flight of steps to the covered porchway, and following him, Delia marvelled at the absolute quietness. The inmates must be home from work, she thought, then she realized they were probably having their evening meal. Inside the house and going through the hall area, Delia noticed rows of pegs which reminded her of her school days.

They passed through the hall to a door at the end of a passageway. As Paddy opened the door a shout of welcome assailed them and Delia found herself blinking in confusion at the crowd of people in the room.

Aunt Lucy in a dark silk dress came forward and caught her arm, then gave her a swift peck on the cheek. 'My, you're getting more like your mother every day!' she exclaimed, and pulled the bewildered Delia forward. 'Now quieten down, everybody,' she ordered the assembly. 'Meet my niece, Miss Delia Dene. Not much of her, I'll admit, but if she's anything like her aunt she'll soon make her presence felt!'

A shout of laughter greeted this remark. A cup of tea was thrust into Delia's hand and, taking it, she tried to collect her thoughts. She had not counted on a welcome like this. Miss Delia Dene! Heavens, now what could she do? Shout that she was married – and widowed? She closed her eyes – she couldn't! Not in front of all these people.

Someone found her a chair, and as she sat down Delia put the tea on a nearby table and made as if searching in her bag for a handkerchief, then slipped her rings off. Her heart whispered an apology to Philip. He would understand. Later, she would tell her aunt. There were tears in her eyes when she raised her head.

Aunt Lucy patted her on the back gently. 'Tired, girl? It's a long way, I know. You drink your tea,' she said, and turned back to the company. 'Now just give her a little while to get her breath and I'll introduce her to you all personally.'

A short while later the introductions began. A tall thin faded-looking woman with sad eyes was the first on the list and introduced by Aunt Lucy as, 'Mary, my help. Don't know what I'd do without her.'

The said Mary looked gratified but muttered, 'You could have fooled me this morning when you bawled me out for forgetting to order the flour!'

There were several people on different committees. Delia lost track half-way through the introductions; she would never remember them, she thought bewilderedly.

At last the evening came to a close. Delia was exhausted and noticed that her aunt was paler than usual, she thought of Paddy's words and when ordered to 'sleep in' the next morning, passed it off with a smile and told her aunt she intended to be up early enough to help with the chores. She was, she assured her, no lady of leisure. For a moment or two it looked as if Aunt Lucy would protest, but she gave in quite suddenly, and this confirmed Delia's suspicions that the evening had taken more out of her than she cared to admit.

By six-thirty the following morning Delia was up and dressed, she knew the girls' breakfast had to be served at seven-thirty, giving them ample time for any last-minute chores before leaving for the factory at eight-twenty.

Venturing down to the kitchen, she was surprised to find no sign of activity. The old stove was unlit, and stacked kindling ready to be piled in lay beside it. Delia stood there eyeing it dubiously and wondered whether she ought to light it. The side door rattled and she found Mary on the doorstep and let her in. Mary stood staring round the kitchen, her glance rested on the unlighted stove.

'Lucy okay?' she asked with raised brows.

Delia knew then that something was wrong; Mary had expected to find the door open and the stove lighted. 'I'll go and see,' she said worriedly, and made for the stairs.

Her heart was thudding as she knocked on her aunt's bedroom door and, not waiting for a reply, went in.

Aunt Lucy sat in one of the chairs. She was fully dressed, but that was as far as she had got. Her hand was pressed to her breast and there was a yellowy look about her, her eyes were closed.

'Aunt Lucy?' Delia said softly. 'You're going back to bed, and no arguing,' she added firmly as she met her aunt's eyes.

She was relieved to see a weak grin, then her aunt sighed. 'Guess I've not much choice,' she conceded. She submitted to Delia's administrations and when back into bed and comfortably settled, she asked, 'Mary here?'

Delia nodded and her aunt gave another sigh. 'Well, she'll get on with things, she knows by now what to do.'

She looked at Delia. 'Sorry, girl; not much of a welcome, is it?'

Her voice did not hold much strength in it, and Delia knew she must be in a certain amount of pain. 'Get old Doc Selby to put me up a potion; he knows what I want. Be right as rain tomorrow, you see,' she muttered.

After making sure Aunt Lucy had everything she needed, Delia made her way back to the kitchen again. There were sounds of movement from the girls' rooms and she guessed they would soon be making their way to the shower rooms. As she entered the kitchen the smell of bacon and eggs drifted towards her; Mary apparently had 'got on with it'.

'What's up, then?' queried Mary, busy at the stove.

Delia told her, and Mary shrugged her shoulders. 'Seen it coming for months,' she said. 'She wouldn't ease up. Weren't nothing you could do about it. You go and phone the doc, I can manage.' Then as Delia reached the door she called, 'Expect she's asked for one of them potions. You take no mind what she says, you get the doc to come and look at her.' She grinned at Delia. 'She's in no position to refuse to see him,' she added wickedly.

Delia nodded, and went to make the call.

In spite of the doctor's cheerful, 'Be right over,' he did not put in an appearance until nine o'clock. In the meantime, Delia took instructions from Mary as to how she could help with the chores.

'Soon as we got breakfast over,' Mary said, 'we can ease off a bit. Any girl late down today's going to be unlucky,' she muttered.

There were twenty girls resident, and by the time Delia had helped with the serving up and pouring out of numerous cups of tea, she felt there ought to be a recount! It had seemed more like forty! She even had time to help Mary with the washing-up after the last girl had rushed down the hostel steps and into the waiting transport, before the doctor arrived.

Doctor Selby was a tubby, jovial man whose thick eyebrows rose when he was informed by Delia that her aunt was in bed. Delia herself was surprised when actually she had to show him which room was her aunt's bedroom. Aunt Lucy, it appeared, had managed to hold him at bay in the past.

Delia was not certain whether she ought to accompany the doctor in, but braved the elements; she had a feeling her aunt would not take too kindly to his visit and she was right. Aunt Lucy, taking one look at him, tried to sit up, but failed, and sank back on to the pillows weakly.

'What do you think you're doing here, Jim Selby?' she demanded. 'No call to come visiting. You put me up some more of that poison. I'll do.'

Taking no notice whatsoever of this belligerent greeting, the doctor walked towards the bed. 'Now, Lucy, I just want to take a look at that chest of yours,' he began. 'I told you this would happen one day, didn't I? That poison as you call it helps, but it's no cure.'

'I don't feel like being mauled around,' said Aunt Lucy pettishly. 'Just let me be.'

Delia stepped forward. 'Aunt Lucy!' she said half scoldingly, half warningly.

Her aunt looked at her, then back to the doctor, then sighed loudly. 'Two against one ain't fair,' she growled, then glared at the doctor. 'Well, what are you waiting for? Get on with it!'

The doctor had a word with Delia before he left. He spoke to her in the privacy of Aunt Lucy's sitting-room and did not beat about the bush. 'It's a duodenal ulcer,' he said abruptly. 'Knowing Lucy, I don't suppose she told you. She's had it for years. With diet and rest she can be cured – rest more than anything else.' He looked at Delia and gave a smile. 'Just out from England, aren't you? Well, I guess you know more about your aunt than I thought you would. She certainly listened to you up there.' His thick brows shot up at Delia. 'I want her in hospital,' he said firmly. 'That way I can control her diet and make her rest. She'll have to be tied to the bed to make her do that if she stays here. Do you think you can persuade her?'

'I'll try,' answered Delia. 'Not that I can guarantee success, but I'll do my best.'

The doctor nodded approvingly. 'Well, I'll go ahead anyway and make arrangements to have her in tomorrow. Have her ready by ten, all right?'

Again Delia agreed, and again she had her doubts. It wouldn't be for want of trying, though. The doctor gave her a pat on the back and left her to it.

Delia stood staring at the closed door wondering just how she was going to break the news to her aunt. Taking a deep breath, she decided there was no time like the present, and she might as well get it over with before she lost her courage.

CHAPTER TWO

Aunt Lucy was sitting up when Delia walked in. Her long hair had been plaited and twisted back into its customary style across her head. Delia thought how like her father she was. There was the same high forehead and strong, almost aggressive features; her dark brown eyes held the same 'I'll say what I think' look. Delia recalled her mother once saying that although Lucy and her brother were fond of each other, there was no living with the pair of them, each liked their own way.

'I feel better already,' declared Aunt Lucy stoutly.

Delia just looked at her, but there was something in that look that made her aunt pull a wry face. 'Right, out with it! What did he say?' she demanded.

'He wants you in hospital,' Delia said quietly. 'And before you start laying the law down I might as well tell you I agree with him.' Seeing her aunt's face set in stubborn resistance, Delia hurried on, 'If you're going to say there's no one to carry on for you, that won't work. I'm here, Mary and I can manage.'

Aunt Lucy gave her an odd considering look. 'Got it all worked out, haven't you?' she said sourly.

'Well, I didn't come all this way to attend your funeral,' answered Delia firmly. 'I want you well, and you need rest, and rest is what you'll get if you're sensible and do what the doctor says.'

To Delia's amazement Aunt Lucy gave a half-weary, 'When?'

'Tomorrow,' replied Delia.

'I'm not promising,' muttered Aunt Lucy. 'We'll see how we go.'

'We'll do no such thing! You're going!' Delia assured her.

Her aunt grinned. 'Said you were like me, didn't I? Ought to be ashamed of yourself, bullying an old woman on her sick-bed!'

Delia grinned back. 'Poor aunt,' she said soothingly.

'You don't get round me like that!'

Delia's grin grew wider, and her aunt patted the bed. 'Come and sit down,' she ordered. 'If you're going to run the show there's a lot I have to tell you. Things have got to be done right. No letting up of the rules, mind you. Late night Saturday. Doors closed at midnight, or locked out. Got that?'

There was a tap on the door at this point, and Mary poked her head round it. 'Brought you some sustenance,' she said, as she entered carrying a tray. Delia hoped it wasn't bacon and eggs, but Mary obviously knew the ropes. There was a bowl of bread and milk and a very weak cup of tea. Delia glanced half apprehensively at her aunt, and to her surprise watched her accept the tray without a murmur.

'Delia's taking over,' Aunt Lucy announced baldly to Mary. 'I'm being rounded up into dock tomorrow.' She stared at Mary as if daring her to make some comment. 'Guess you two will get along okay. You'll work for Delia, won't you, Mary?'

Delia protested, 'Mary knows much more than I do. I'll take orders from her.'

'Mary's no organizer,' Aunt Lucy said firmly, adding as an afterthought, 'Good cook, though.'

Mary agreed with this statement proudly. 'No good asking me to give orders. I couldn't organize a bunfight. No, you run the show like Lucy says. We'll make out.'

That settled, Mary left to start the chores.

Aunt Lucy went back to her instruction. 'As I was saying,' she said, as she stirred some of the milky sop on to a spoon, 'time's time. And maybe a few will try it on seeing as you're new, but you show 'em what's what. I've been running this place for twenty years and folk know when their girls come to me they get looked after. No hokey-pokey. Might seem a mite old-fashioned to you, but this isn't England. Nothing doing around these parts after midnight – any girl about then is up to no good. We got a clean licence and Dane sees it's kept that way.'

Delia, waiting until her aunt had swallowed most of her sparse meal, wondered who Dane was; probably the local law officer, she surmised.

'So,' continued Aunt Lucy, 'ten-thirty's the time weekdays, twelve Saturday. The girls usually go to a local hop at the farm, there's not much else to do. I don't do no rounds to see if lights are out, most of 'em work hard and are too tired to stay up and burn the midnight oil.' She drank some of her tea. 'There's some books in the office, I'll get you to bring them up to me and I'll show you what to do. Have to keep a register, of course. There's no new girls expected, but you might get a few inquiries. They've got to have a legitimate reason for coming to the district, there's a lot of well-paid bachelors around and it attracts the drifters on the look-out for a well-heeled husband. We don't aim to take any of those in. If they haven't got a job with one of the local industries, then it's no go. If they say they're looking for work, you don't take them until you get the okay from whoever they say had employed them. Saves a lot of trouble in the long run.'

So the day progressed for Delia, most of it spent with Aunt Lucy receiving instructions. It wasn't until after Delia had helped serve the evening meal at six that she had time for personal thought. Her aunt was still unaware of her marriage, and it didn't seem the right time to bring it up. She sighed as she wiped the dishes. There was plenty of time, she was not going anywhere. It was something that could wait until Aunt Lucy was well again.

By the end of the week Delia had found her feet. She was on nodding acquaintance with most of the girls and was addressed as 'Miss Dene'. Their ages ranged between seventeen and nineteen, and Delia, at twenty-five, felt quite matronly. At first they had been a little shy with her, but on closer acquaintance became more forthcoming.

Soon Delia found herself in the dual role of confidante and stand-in mum. She had no objection to this role. A naturally shy person, she had found it hard to make friends, but now it appeared she was being forced out of her shell. She had no time for looking back and dwelling on what might have been; her own heart-aches were shelved in listening to others' problems, and she was grateful for being kept busy. An odd sensation of 'coming home' pervaded her being, and although she did not quite understand it, she was happy.

At the end of the second week, she began to see why Aunt Lucy had been tired. It was a vast house, and although the girls kept their own rooms clean, it still left a lot to be done, quite apart from the preparing and serving of meals each day. There was no other help but Mary who cooked and cleaned, but Mary could not manage the cleaning on her own and like Aunt Lucy, Delia set to and did her share, but it was hard going — everything was so antiquated.

The large lounge for the residents needed refurnishing, the present covers on the settees and chairs, though clean, were threadbare. The long window curtains were in the same state. There were patches of wear on the carpet, and the lounge was only one room needing attention. The shower rooms Delia surmised to be the very first of their type, and there were only three, not really enough for the amount of girls resident; the water supply was erratic too, proving to Delia that the whole plumbing system needed an overhaul.

Noting these things, she came to the conclusion that either the hostel had not paid for itself, or Aunt Lucy had not bothered to move with the times.

She sighed as she collected the used towels from the shower rooms. For the first time since her widowhood she wished she had stood up to Philip's sister and aunt. John had told her that although Philip had not made a recent will, or if he had, no trace of it had been found, she was still entitled to claim part of the estate as his wife. She had been horrified at the thought of contesting the will, she had been too heartsick and crushed by his death to want any mercenary compensation. For her own sake she still did not want it, but what a help it would have been now, when she thought of the use she could have put it to, and Philip would have wanted that, too. It was not as if his relations were destitute; they were exceedingly well off, but determined Delia should not inherit.

That Saturday Delia visited Aunt Lucy. The hospital was five miles away from the township, and Delia had to make the journey by bus. The hostel had no transport of its own but relied on the farm for transport when necessary. There were quite a few things, Delia reflected as she got on the bus, that the hostel had to rely on from Marrabee; the Saturday hop was only one. From the farm came the fruit for the canning factories and the sole prosperity of the town. As yet Delia had seen little of the district, but Mary had told her about the acres and acres of orchard that made up Marrabee. 'A prettier sight you couldn't see,' she had said.

As Delia had feared, Aunt Lucy was better but fretful. 'Never been so idle for so long in all my life,' she complained after Delia had given her a hug and handed her the magazines she had brought her.

Considering this was only the first week, and there were two more weeks to go, Delia reminded her to make the most of her enforced holiday, but Aunt Lucy all but snorted at the thought.

'I'm a fraud,' she declared. 'They must be short of customers to drag me in. As for peace, there's more on a railway station! No sooner do I settle down for a snooze than I've a visitor. Every durn committee in town's sent someone to find out if I'm ready to hand in my meal ticket!'

Delia chuckled, but felt relieved, she had imagined Aunt Lucy being the only one without visitors as the evening visiting hours coincided with the hostel's meal, and Delia had been unable to visit her before the week-end.

When it was time to go, Aunt Lucy told her not to bother about coming the next day. 'Have a few hours to yourself, girl; you've earned it. I'll see you next week.'

Delia's step was light as she walked back to the bus stop. Aunt Lucy had not demanded to be let out; she had grumbled, yes, but Delia suspected she was enjoying herself holding court, as it were, in the hospital ward. It wouldn't surprise her a tiny bit to find her aunt had reorganized the whole hospital procedure before she left.

There was an air of excited expectancy in the hostel that evening, it was the night of the hop at Marrabee. The dance had been cancelled the previous Saturday because of the press of work, much to the disappointment of the few remaining girls having to spend the week-ends at the hostel. Of the twenty residents about a dozen were able to get home for the week-ends, so in actual fact although there were not as many to cater for, the week-end brought no respite from the daily chores. Delia wondered whether Aunt Lucy ever had a holiday, and marvelled that she had lasted as long as she had. Mary finished at lunchtime on Saturdays, until the following Monday, leaving a cold collation for the girls' meal on Sunday.

As Delia sat sewing some frayed sheet ends in her aunt's sitting-room, she listened to the hurried preparations and giggles coming from the girls' quarters. Twice she had been sought out for help in emergencies; once a stuck zip that no one could shift, and on the second occasion to provide a pink coloured silk cotton to tack up a frill that had detached itself at the last moment.

There was a hooting outside and then a mad rush down the stairs, then perfect peace. Delia sat back and listened to the sound of silence. For the first time since her arrival she was alone, the evening was hers to do as she wished. Remembering her loneliness in England after Philip's death, and how she had longed for someone to relieve her solitude, Delia never thought at that time an evening of peace would be welcomed, but here she was, thankful for the brief respite an empty house gave her.

When she had finished the sewing, she found herself a novel from the bookcase in the lounge and settled down to read it. She became so immersed in the story she did not notice the hands of the clock slip round, and when she next glanced at it the hands were close to midnight. Delia frowned; there was no sign of the girls. Would the van arrive sharp on the hour? There were still a few minutes to go, she half-smiled; perhaps they had got it down to a fine art!

However, when it was a quarter past the hour, and still no sign of them, Delia began to worry. Aunt Lucy told her the farm people were reliable and never kept the girls past time. At twenty past, she was considering ringing the local law officer, if she remembered rightly someone called Dane, her aunt had mentioned. Going downstairs to the hall telephone, she searched through the directory for local numbers trying to locate the name, but had no success. The Marrabee number was there, however, so she tried that, but there was no reply.

By this time Delia had convinced herself there had been a serious accident and the girls were lying injured in a ditch somewhere. Why hadn't she been told what to do in an emergency? At the end of her tether, she was about to put her coat on and go in search of someone to advise her what to do, when she heard the sound of a motor coming down the drive.

She rushed to the door and stood watching the van draw up in front of the house, her anxiety giving way to untold relief as she saw the girls alight one by one from the van assisted by the driver. They did not seem at all frightened or upset. In fact, they were in the best of spirits, if their giggles were anything to go by.

As Delia watched these proceedings, her relief turned to quite another emotion, cold rage. Not one of them looked a bit contrite, and to think she had nearly worried herself silly over them!

The girls filed past her and into the hall where Delia stood silently awaiting an explanation. The driver, an extremely tall man, sauntered towards her. He appeared to be somewhat amused and grinned at Delia. 'Sorry, ma'am, we kinda broke down.'

For a moment or so Delia was too angry to say anything, then she saw one of the girls sway and cling to her companion. Delia's eyes widened. 'Are those girls drunk?' she demanded. 'I was given to understand only soft drinks were served at the dance.'

The man found this amusing as well. 'Ran out of soft drinks, I expect. Won't hurt 'em, I guess they tried the iced beer.'

Delia found her voice, she even surprised herself – she did not think she had it in her! She verbally tore into the man like a small tornado, certain now it had been a 'try-on'. If they thought she was going to stand for that they had another think coming!

The man's eyes widened in shock as she laid the law down. Amongst other things that he could tell the organizers of the dance that the girls would not be attending any future functions unless an assurance was given that this episode would not be repeated – and furthermore, she would expect an apology from someone in the very near future.

Beyond words, the stunned man touched his hat and hastily left.

Delia then looked at the girls standing staring in disbelief at the normally placid Delia. One held her hand to her mouth. 'I feel sick,' she said, and rushed up the stairs.

Three of the eight girls were sick that night, and Delia, administering to them, was extremely tired the next morning when she delivered her first lecture.

CHAPTER THREE

DELIA was grateful it was Sunday. After she had delivered her lecture the girls apologized, Meg, the youngest, saying, 'We oughtn't to have tried the beer. It was quite nice really,' she added musingly, then frowned. 'But I won't try it again. I've never been so sick before.'

Well, at least one lesson had been learnt, Delia thought tiredly, and not only by the girls, she hoped.

The rest of the day passed peacefully. There had been no apology from Marrabee, and Delia would have relented her decision to ban the next dance had there been one; as it was, she stood by her decision.

After the evening meal, the girls offered to help with the washing-up, and a little surprised, Delia accepted. This, she realized, was their way of saying sorry.

All the chores finished, she settled down in her sitting-room, this time to make out a list of provisions for the coming week's meals. There were past lists to guide her, and all she had to do was prepare a new list and phone it through to the local grocer the following morning and have it sent down.

There was a tap on the door, and Delia, thinking it was one of the girls wanting something, called out, 'I won't be a moment.'

To her surprise the door opened. Whoever it was had no intention of waiting for her to open the door. Delia stared at the man facing her. He was tallish, of lean build, and red-headed. His hat was pushed to the back of his head, but it was his eyes that held her attention. They were a startling blue, more so probably, because of his deep tan. Eyes that wouldn't miss much, she thought, as she saw him taking her in, every inch of her. As she noticed his immaculate tan shirt and fawn slacks, the thought flashed through her mind that this man was no ordinary farmhand.

'Who the devil are you?' he demanded in a soft southern drawl.

Delia felt as if she had been put under a fine microscope, and not liking it, answered in the same vein. 'I might ask you the same question,' she said coldly.

One autocratic eyebrow raised at this reply, then he said abruptly, 'Sinclair.'

He did not offer to shake hands, Delia noticed, although she now knew she was talking to the boss of Marrabee. She wondered if this omission was supposed to put her in her place. He stood waiting, that one eyebrow still raised.

Delia brushed an imaginary speck off her cashmere sweater and said, 'For want of a better name, housemother.'

For a second he said nothing, but his eyes narrowed as he silently acknowledged the snub, then he drawled, 'Well, housemother, perhaps you'd be good enough to explain why you thought it necessary to bawl my foreman out last night and ban next week's dance?'

Delia just stared at him, but before she could answer, he asked curtly, 'Where's Lucy?' in a tone of voice that clearly stated he couldn't be bothered with the likes of her.

'In hospital,' Delia answered promptly. 'I'm afraid you'll have to deal with me, Mr. Sinclair.' She was about to explain in no uncertain terms why she had refused to allow the girls to attend the dance, when he shot another question at her.

'What's the connection?'

'I beg your pardon?' she said icily.

He sighed as if deciding he had an idiot to deal with. 'Lucy wouldn't leave things in the hands of a complete stranger,' he said slowly. 'So I'll ask you again. What's the connection?'

'I don't see what business that is of yours,' Delia replied angrily.

He took a deep breath. 'The name's Sinclair, ma'am,' he said softly. 'This is my town, if you want to play it that way. Any other questions?'

So what? thought Delia. Aunt Lucy owned the hostel, didn't she? She looked at this autocratic man waiting her answer. 'None,' she said crisply.

'Good,' he said in mock relief. 'Now for the last time, who are you?'

Delia bit her lip, feeling cornered. 'Her niece,' she said haughtily, her eyes showing her feelings.

'Ah, yes, the English girl,' he drawled. 'Well, niece, let me give you some good advice. This is a hostel, not a detention centre. I shall expect the girls to attend the next hoe-down. Do we understand each other?'

Delia did not reply, she was too furious.

'It's surprising, isn't it?' he went on conversationally, 'how being in charge goes to some people's heads.'

Delia flushed. Of all the snide remarks! Okay, if he wanted a fight he could have one! Her eyes sparked.

'I'm in an unenviable position, Mr. Sinclair,' she said, matching his drawling tone. 'There are twenty girls under my care. Admittedly, only eight attended the dance last night, but they didn't get back until way past midnight.'

He gave an impatient shrug. 'A perfectly good explanation was given for their late arrival,' he said coldly, as if Delia were making a fuss about nothing.

'It wasn't only their late arrival,' she said quietly, determined to hold on to her temper. 'Several of the girls were intoxicated. I suspect the van was overdue because of several, shall we say, unexpected stops?'

To her fury, he grinned. 'Now there I do admit we were at fault. I heard the soft drinks ran out. It was a very hot night, if you remember. It will not occur again. Incidentally,' he shot her a look of authority, 'there was no need to tear my foreman off a strip. Any complaints, I deal with. Got that? They're my men and answerable only to me.'

The message was given slowly to enable Delia to get the full implication. She did, and it didn't exactly make for good relations.

'So,' he went on, 'they come next week, okay?' It was not so much a question as an order.

Delia's lips set. 'I'm sorry,' she said stiffly, 'I've told them they will not be attending next week. Perhaps the following week.'

His eyes narrowed. 'Poor little devils,' he murmured softly. 'You do realize it's about the only outing they get, don't you? If you don't trust them out of your sight why don't you come with them? You can always sit with Cooky and vet the food. Forget your exalted position for once. I don't want any kill-joys around.'

Delia's eyes blazed. 'Is that an order?' she ground out.

He grinned wickedly. 'On which count?' he asked lazily. 'The dance, or your attendance?'

Delia took a deep breath. He was being deliberately provocative. 'The dance,' she said icily. 'My free time is my own. I have no wish to spend it at Marrabee.'

His coldness matched hers. 'You wouldn't be exactly welcome at that. I should imagine the girls would be relieved to spend an evening without their watchdog.' He strode towards the door. 'They'll be collected at the usual time,' he said harshly, and stamped out.

Delia stood for a long time in the middle of the floor. She badly wanted to hit out at something, anything; preferably Mr. High-and-mighty Sinclair! If being in charge had gone to anybody's head it had certainly gone to his, she thought bitterly. The way he'd said he owned the town! How exalted could you get? Statements like that could reasonably be expected of an older man, but he was in his early thirties, younger, she suspected, than Philip had been. Perhaps he had just taken over and was throwing his weight about? She shrugged; he wasn't worth getting upset about – as for the girls attending the next dance – Delia's lips set. As Aunt Lucy would have put it, 'We'll see.'

The following morning Delia recounted the incident to Mary. At the mention of the name Sinclair, Mary pricked her ears up. 'Dane? He's back, then?' she asked quickly.

Delia paused and stared at her. 'Dane?' she repeated.

Mary's brows rose. 'There's only one Sinclair,' she

said. 'Although I don't know anyone who calls him that, it's just Dane.'

Delia digested this news silently. He was Mr. to her, and always would be! She continued the narration, and when she had finished, Mary looked amused, Delia felt exasperated; everyone but her seemed to find it amusing!

'Well, if Dane had been there the girls wouldn't have got at the beer,' Mary commented. 'I wouldn't mind betting someone got torn off a strip for that. Dane don't hold with that sort of thing. I guess he must have got back on Sunday.'

In spite of herself, Delia was curious. 'Doesn't he live at Marrabee, then?' she asked.

'Course!' retorted Mary. 'But he does a lot of travelling around. London, Paris, New York. A lot of the canned fruit is exported, you know.'

Big business, Delia thought sourly. 'Has he always owned Marrabee?' she asked casually.

Mary seemed surprised at the question. 'Since he was in his teens,' she replied. 'Good thing for the town he does. He's built that business up. The factories weren't there in his father's day.' She shot Delia a sly look. 'Now, don't you go getting interested in our most eligible bachelor. You'll have to join a queue – all the females are after him, and it's not just because he's rich either, if you know what I mean. He's no ladies' man, though – might give a pretty girl a whirl, but that's as far as it gets. I wouldn't exactly call him a heartbreaker – but there's plenty wishing he'd look their way.'

Delia was horrified at the thought of being classed as one of his admirers. 'For my part the whole town's welcome to him!' she said sourly, and stalked out of the kitchen, leaving Mary gaping after her.

A few days later the subject of the dance cropped up again, Delia asked Mary if it was true there was no other entertainment for the girls. Mary gave the same answer as Dane Sinclair, then looked at Delia. 'You're not going to stop them going, are you?' she asked. 'Might mean trouble for Lucy, you know. If Dane says they're going, then they're going, in spite of what you say. He's chairman of the welfare committee and these dances were run specially to give the girls some sort of break.'

'We'll see what Aunt Lucy says,' said Delia obstinately.

Mary stared at her. 'Whatever Dane says goes for Lucy too,' she declared emphatically. 'Thinks the world of Dane, does Lucy. He's the only one she'll listen to when she gets pigheaded. Anything the committee want to change and know they'll have trouble convincing Lucy – he's the one they get to talk her round – and he always does!'

Delia could have screamed; it was like coming up against a brick wall and there was no sense in banging her head against it. As the week-end neared, she became resigned to the fact that the girls would attend the dance, and she would have to go back on her previous statement and tell them they were free to go if they wished. In a way she was relieved; she hadn't liked the thought of denying them their only outing, especially as they had apologized, and there was no fear of a repetition of the beer incident. She did wish she could have found some alternative pleasure for

32

them just so they wouldn't be beholden to Dane Sinclair.

She had managed to thrust him out of her mind for several days when she was forced to undertake another confrontation. The task, to say the least, was delicate and Delia would have given anything not to have had to tackle it.

It was a rule of the hostel that anyone calling for one of the girls, be it male or female, should make their presence known to Aunt Lucy, also where they intended spending the evening. At first, Delia had smiled when she came across this stipulation in the rule book. Surely she wasn't expected to carry that rule out? Although, she mused, as Aunt Lucy had pointed out, this was not England and the girls were young and away from home. Nevertheless, Delia couldn't see herself demanding to know where the intended dates meant to escort the girls. Aunt Lucy could, and very probably did. Delia decided to content herself with the name of the young man only.

However, when one of the girls knocked on her sitting-room door one evening and announced with a certain amount of envy in her voice, 'Mr. Sinclair has called for Meg, Miss Dene,' Delia did a rapid amendment of her earlier resolve.

Bearing in mind Mary's words about Dane Sinclair 'Giving a pretty girl a whirl', she frowned. Meg was a very pretty girl, she was also a very young girl. Why hadn't she mentioned that she knew Dane Sinclair? Of all the girls in Delia's charge Meg was the closest. She had arrived at the hostel only a day earlier than Delia had. It was the first time Meg had been away from home and she had been very homesick. Delia had gone out of her way to make sure she settled in. Her frown deepened; she wondered how Dane Sinclair could have met Meg in the first place, then she remembered Meg was employed in one of the canning factories offices – and the factories were owned by Dane Sinclair! Simple really, she thought, only it wasn't a bit simple! Why on earth had he picked on Meg? There were several girls much more his stamp, she would have thought.

Delia tightened her lips; this time she would carry out the rules of the house! Half-way down the stairs, she knew an irresistible urge to turn tail and let the devil take the hindmost! Then she upbraided herself for being a coward. Meg, after all, was not quite seventeen.

Dane Sinclair was standing in Aunt Lucy's small office off the hall. No waiting in the hall where ordinary mortals wait, for him, Delia thought crossly. He stood idly flicking over the pages of a magazine that lay on the table. On this occasion he was not wearing a hat, and Delia noticed that his red hair was not too long, slightly curly and expertly cut; she had to admit grudgingly to herself that she liked it. She even approved of the suit he wore. As before, he was immaculately turned out. The cream linen suit and pale blue silk shirt looked made to measure. He looked bigger than she had remembered. Delia swallowed. 'Mr. Sinclair?' she said, as she neared him.

He looked up then, and did not answer right away, but took his time surveying her. It was a calculated pause to put her at a disadvantage and Delia knew it.

She received the distinct impression that she ought to have sought permission before addressing him. Her courage almost deserted her, but she stuck to her guns. She was carrying out the rules of the house, wasn't she?

Still studying her with an almost insolent gaze from those unusual eyes of his, he said abruptly, 'Yes?'

Delia decided to go in the deep end; he was not a man who would appreciate subterfuge. 'I understand you are escorting Meg Graham this evening,' she said firmly, meeting his eyes, and noting the sudden start and the tightening of his strong jaw.

'Yes—?' he drawled slowly.

Feeling an urge to slap that arrogant face, Delia took a deep breath. 'Please don't think I'm interfering,' she said quickly, 'but Meg is rather young, you know, and rather impressionable ...' She faltered a little, not liking the look in his eyes. 'As I believe I have explained to you before, I do have some responsibility towards the girls ...' She broke off lamely. Wretched man, she thought, he knows very well what I'm getting at, and yet he lets me flounder. It made her all the more determined. 'May I ask you to see she gets back at ten-thirty sharp?' she asked, then paused; surely he had got the message now? If he didn't like it, and if his expression was anything to go by, he didn't; there was nothing Delia could do about it.

'But you are interfering, aren't you?' he said softly.

Delia started. No, he hadn't liked it one bit, and she sighed inwardly; having come so far, she wasn't going to give up now. 'I'm sorry to be a spoilsport,' she murmured, 'but most of the girls can look after themselves. Meg is different.' She found herself desperately wishing she could make him understand. 'I just don't want her hurt, that's all,' she finished lamely.

Dane Sinclair studied her silently for a second or so. 'You don't believe in pulling your punches, do you?' he drawled, with an undercurrent of fury in his voice. 'Do you enjoy your work, Miss Dene?' he taunted.

So he knew her name now, she thought idly, as she decided there was no further point in going on with the conversation, and walked towards the door.

'Of course you do,' he continued smoothly. 'Were your dreams wrecked, Miss Dene? Is that why you take your duties so seriously? Mother confessor to a bunch of females is right up your street, isn't it?' He noted her quick flush. 'So I was right, was I? All men are poison, are they? All out to snare your little ewe lambs? Why don't you let your hair down? I'm sure you envy them their good times. Hearing about it secondhand isn't the same, you know,' he said silkily. 'You can get frustrated that way. Life will get distorted if you keep on denying yourself. You're not bad-looking, you might attract someone. Of course,' he paused deliberately, 'you'll have to smile occasionally and make an attempt to be pleasant, but I'm sure with a little practice you can make it.'

Delia was shocked. Her eyes spoke her thoughts.

'Go on,' he urged softly, 'you're starting to be human. Slap my face – it will do you good, get rid of that frustration I was telling you about.'

For one awful moment Delia very nearly did as he suggested, then she drew a deep breath, and when she could trust herself to speak she said quietly, 'I'm sorry, however much I'd like to oblige, I must deny myself that pleasure. If you would excuse me.' She turned to go.

When she reached the door, the drawling voice spoke again. 'Miss Dene? Meg happens to be a daughter of a friend of mine, and as such will come to no harm.'

Delia did not wait to hear any more, but made her way back to her quarters.

On the stairs, she passed Denise, a tall willowy blonde, and noticed she was dressed to create an impression. Delia could guess her intention. It would be all round the hostel that Dane Sinclair had called. 'Going out, Denise?' she asked.

The girl paused dramatically, and turned to face her. 'I might,' she said, then added, 'if anything turns up.'

The 'anything', Delia guessed, being asked to accompany Dane Sinclair and Meg to whatever destination he had in mind. Denise, she was sure, would know of the connection between Meg and that man. There was not much Denise would not know. If anyone was looking for a well-heeled husband, Denise was. Delia had wondered why she had cultivated Meg; now all was explained.

Delia moved on up the stairs; she only wished she had known, too. It would have saved her from a most embarrassing interview.

Reaching the landing, she met Meg coming out of her room. She wore a pretty silk printed dress, her dark curly hair framed her heart-shaped face, and wide brown eyes that emphasized her youth smiled at Delia.

'Very nice,' Delia said softly, noting with approval

that Meg had not as yet adopted eye make-up; her eyes needed no highlighting. 'Why didn't you tell me you knew Dane Sinclair?' she asked, half-scoldingly.

Meg looked anxious. 'Well,' she said, in her forth-right way, 'I did mention it when I first came here, but everyone thought I was showing off, and I didn't want you to think so, too, so I didn't say anything.'

Delia smiled and ruffled Meg's curls. 'You ought to know me better than that,' she scolded her affectionately.

Meg looked relieved, and grinned.

'Have a good time!' Delia called as Meg rushed down the stairs.

Reaching her room, Delia closed the door with a thankful sigh, and leant back against it. She had not realized how shaken she was; her knees were weak and her hands shaking. A dull flush crept over her cheeks as she recalled the scene in the office. How dared Dane Sinclair say such things!

She walked shakily forward to the small oval mirror on the wall, and gazed at herself critically. Did she look like a dried-up spinster? And that bit about letting her hair down! She sighed; scraping her hair back in that severe bun did, she supposed, give that impression, but she had meant it to. With her hair loose, framing her face, she looked no older than the girls she was looking after.

Frowning at her reflection, she pulled the pins out of her hair and shook it back to the way she used to wear it, in soft waves framing her face. There was no doubt about it, it did lessen the impact of those high cheek-bones of hers, and gave her a softer appearance.

Meeting her eyes in the mirror, she gave a grimace; what did it matter what Dane Sinclair thought? If he thought she looked grim, well, she'd look grim! And as for smiling more often – her lips straightened, and she pushed her hair firmly back into the bun style, then looked around for something to do to take her mind off the evening's incident, and was soon applying herself once more to the frayed sheets.

At ten o'clock, she put the work away, and went down to the lounge to clear up the cups and saucers from the girls' late-night drink. With a loaded tray, she passed from the lounge to the hall towards the kitchen, and was just passing the main door when a sardonic voice spoke close at hand.

'Not tucked up yet, Miss Dene? Or are you checking to see all your chicks have come home to roost? Tell me, do you tuck them all up at night?'

'Dane!' exclaimed Meg in a shocked voice.

Delia wouldn't lower herself to answer this jibe – she smiled at Meg. 'Had a good time?' she asked, and walked on.

'A moment, please, Miss Dene,' Dane Sinclair requested as he followed Meg into the hall.

Delia glanced at him, and her brows lifted; it was late and no visitors were allowed after ten. She glanced meaningly at the clock.

'I know the rules as well as you do,' he said curtly. 'In case you don't know, I'm chairman of the hostel welfare committee, and in that capacity I want to have a few words with you – if you've no objection.'

Delia was thinking they must be hard up for senior citizens if they had to depend on him for chairmanship.

She saw him smile, and it was not a pleasant smile; she hazarded a guess that he had sensed her thoughts, and his next words proved it.

'I don't seem the type, do I?' he drawled. 'However, that's as maybe. I've taken it on, and you'll have to put up with me.'

There was another shocked exclamation from Meg, standing wide-eyed beside him. 'Dane!'

'Go to bed,' he said briefly to her, in a voice that meant exactly what it said.

Meg looked despondent and started for the stairs.

Dane Sinclair looked back at Delia. 'I hear you have not as yet told the girls the dance is on again,' he said curtly.

Half-way up the stairs, Meg broke in with, 'I didn't want to get you into trouble, Miss Dene.'

'Are you going?' Dane Sinclair demanded of Meg. 'Or am I going to carry you up those stairs?'

'I'm going,' Meg said hastily, and went.

Delia's tray was getting heavy, but he had not offered to relieve her of it, she noticed. 'Do you mind if I get rid of this?' she asked in a voice meant to convey what she thought of his manners.

'Not a bit,' he replied casually. 'Don't you have any domestics?'

'They're off duty,' she replied sharply. He must have known there was only Mary, anyway.

She carried the tray into the kitchen, and to her annoyance Dane Sinclair followed her. She placed the tray on the kitchen table, then said coldly, 'Would you come through to the office, please?'

'I don't see why we need move from here,' he announced grandly. 'Or are you playing for time?'

Delia's eyes flashed. Really, he was the pink limit! 'I am not playing for time,' she snapped, then made an effort to hold her temper in check. 'I shall tell them tomorrow. In fact, I shall pin a notice up on the board as well. Does that satisfy you?' she asked, adding bitterly, 'It's not as if they had anywhere else to go, is it?'

He studied her. 'Hurts, does it?' he said softly. 'Having to knuckle down, I mean?'

To Delia's fury, she felt the warmth flood her face. 'Is that all you wished to see me about, Mr. Sinclair?' she said icily.

He smiled mockingly. 'All for now, Miss Dene. I mustn't keep you from your beauty sleep, must I?' He walked to the door, but paused when he reached it, and turned back to her. 'Thought any more about joining your charges on Saturday? I'm sure we could fit you in somewhere.'

Delia was beyond answering. She deliberately turned her back on him and started to get on with the washing-up of the crockery. She heard a low chuckle before the door was closed.

CHAPTER FOUR

On Saturday morning, Delia received a letter from home; it was from John. He was the only one she had given her address, as he was handling the selling of her house. Having decided to join her aunt, Delia also decided it would be a clean break; she had no friends close enough to keep up constant correspondence with, and for this she was thankful.

It had given her quite a start seeing the scrawled name on the envelope 'Mrs. P. Courtenay'. Again, she was thankful for the rules of the house, for no one was allowed to touch the post except Aunt Lucy, who would distribute what letters there were for the girls at breakfast time. Delia knew how quickly news could travel in a small township, and would have hated Aunt Lucy to have heard about her marriage from outside sources.

Delia sorted the rest of the mail, and thrust her envelope in her cardigan pocket. She would read it later when the meal was over, and she could retire to her room.

When the chores were finished, she slipped upstairs to her sitting-room and settled down to read her mail. After hoping she was well and settling down in her new environment, John told her he had sold the house, Delia's eyes widened at the price he had obtained for it. He went on to urge her once more to contest the will. She had only to say the word, and he would get things going.

Delia sighed, and looked away from the letter, to the shabby furnishings of her aunt's furniture, then straightened her lips. No – even if she were penniless, she couldn't go through with it; she could well imagine some of the arguments Philip's sister and aunt would put forward, she shuddered; they were welcome to the estate if it meant so much to them. She went back to the letter. John went on to tell her he was thinking of spending part of his next vacation in that part of the world, and would look her up.

Delia's eyes moistened. Dear John, he wanted to make sure she was happy. Her eyes dwelt on that bold signature at the close of the letter 'John Courtenay'. In her mind's eye she saw him again. He was very like Philip, fair, with aquiline features, and the same dark blue eyes.

John was two years older than Philip, and Delia had often wondered why he had not married; he had the looks to attract the opposite sex. Philip had once commented that he was too 'fastidious', and given her a loving embrace, 'As I was, my love, until I had you in my sights.' Delia blinked quickly, and hastily folded the letter back into the envelope.

She sat for a while lost in thought. She had almost forgotten about the money from the sale of the house. Now she could help her aunt out; it wasn't a fortune, and would probably prove only a drop in the ocean when she thought of the many things that wanted putting right in that large establishment – still, the most important things could be done. Delia frowned. One day Aunt Lucy would have to retire, and some of the money must be put aside for that eventuality. Housing and land were no less expensive here than at home. She shrugged; they'd think about that when the time came.

That afternoon Delia visited Aunt Lucy again. She decided not to mention her skirmishes with Dane Sinclair, working on the principle of the least said, the soonest mended, and when her aunt pointed to a huge bunch of red roses on the other side of the room, telling her proudly who had sent them, she was glad she had held her tongue.

'Had them put there,' said Aunt Lucy, 'so I could see 'em. Don't get a proper look at them stuck bang next to me on the locker.'

Delia hastily changed the subject by giving her all the hostel news; not that there was much to report, as all was going well. Delia was half surprised to find her aunt quite resigned to her stay. Neither did she demand to know when she was being 'let out'. Delia suspected the doctor had at last got through to her; she knew the X-rays had shown it had been a near thing. The ulcer would have erupted, had her aunt insisted on carrying on.

Originally, the doctor had said a month's rest, but had since lengthened it to six weeks. He had also told Delia that her aunt's working days would have to be strictly supervised. 'She's just got to learn to take things easy,' he had said, adding with a wry smile, 'I guess you'll have to figure out a way to keep her quiet.' Delia had assured him she would think of something.

Now, as she made her way back to the hostel, Delia wondered just how this could be done. If only Aunt Lucy would agree to give up the hostel, they could move out to a smaller house, and Delia could get a job.

On second thoughts, she decided it would be better if she could persuade Aunt Lucy to move right out of the vicinity; that way she wouldn't have to worry about obtaining a job not connected with the Sinclair hierarchy. Delia didn't want any hand-outs from him!

That evening the girls went to the dance. Delia would not have been surprised if Dane Sinclair had collected them himself, just to rub the point in; however, he had a much more subtle way of making his views known.

The girls returned precisely at ten to twelve. Not only did they return earlier than expected, but the tall driver of the van, known now to her as Dane Sinclair's foreman, presented himself before her after the girls trooped in, and keeping an extremely wary eye on her, he announced, 'All aboard, ma'am,' adding afterwards, 'And sober!' with a wicked grin.

Delia might have thought it funny too, had she not known who was behind the cryptic message. She had no doubt in her mind that the foreman had been instructed to give her that precise message. 'Thank you,' she said quietly. 'Would you tell Mr. Sinclair I much appreciate his thoughtfulness on my account.' And let him see what change he can get out of that! she thought.

The foreman raised his brows at this slightly loaded answer, then touched his hat and left.

The news broke the following week. Delia had taken a particularly persistent defaulter to task about overstepping the time limit. Three nights in a row were a little much even for Della's easygoing management.

45

'Oh, well,' the girl had commented defiantly, 'I won't be here much longer. And I won't be the only one moving. There's a new hostel opening up the other side of town, and they're giving passes every night until midnight. Everything's modern and it'll be heavenly not to wait in a queue for the showers every morning!' She had then flounced off, leaving Delia frowning after her.

Surely it couldn't be true, Delia thought. Aunt Lucy would have heard about it, if it were – besides, you couldn't just open a hostel, you had to have the town committee's approval first. If the new hostel was all modern as the girl had hinted, it must have been built recently and in a town that size the news would have got around. Had the girl heard some rumour and assumed the rest? Delia shrugged, and put it out of her mind.

Towards the end of the week the matter was brought sharply into focus again. Ten of the girls announced their intention of leaving in a fortnight's time, all more or less repeating what had been said before, the new hostel was bang up to date, etc. . . .

A very worried Delia was forced to take some action before she visited Aunt Lucy the following day, so she rang up Mrs. Symes, a prominent member of the town committee. Deciding it was no use hedging, she asked straight out about the new hostel.

Mrs. Symes was very contrite. 'My dear, didn't anyone let you know? Oh, dear, I expect it was a case of everyone thinking someone else had done so. I do apologize. But the need was there,' she explained. 'Lucy isn't getting any younger, you know, and with

46

this new factory opening shortly more girls will be looking for lodgings — so when Dane suggested we take over the Gazelle, well, I mean, it was too good an offer to refuse.'

When Mrs. Symes had got through singing the praises of their worthy chairman, and his generosity in offering his new motel on the outskirts of town as the new hostel, Delia quietly thanked her, and put the receiver down.

Well, she had wondered how she was going to make Aunt Lucy ease up, it didn't look as if she was going to have much trouble in that line now. The town committee had done it for her! But what a way to do it! she thought furiously. They had certainly got a move on — by the time she was out of hospital it would be all over. Aunt Lucy would be returning to an empty hostel. Delia's hands clenched. The hostel was her aunt's sole income, but did they care? Did Dane Sinclair care? If it hadn't been for him, she thought bitterly, they wouldn't have been able to go ahead.

She stared round the small office, and sighed. Like the rest of the house, everything was hopelessly out of date. The ancient typewriter stuttered if one attempted to type more than twenty words a minute. It would have come sooner or later, she thought, but she just wished it hadn't come in quite that way, not with Aunt Lucy's hands tied behind her back, as it were.

Changing into a pale linen dress the following day, Delia mentally rehearsed how she would tell her aunt about the new hostel. Placing her straw hat on her head, she grimaced at her reflection. Of course, she could just come out with, 'They've put you out to grass,

47

Aunt.' It would be no less than the truth, she thought, as she picked up her bag and went downstairs to collect the flowers Mary had brought for Aunt Lucy. Having neatly bunched the flowers, she then collected the few magazines and a local paper she had kept for her aunt, and let herself out of the front door. She had just closed it behind her when a Jaguar drew up. There was only one person who would own such a car, and she found Dane Sinclair giving her a caustic appraisal. As he hadn't spoken, Delia presumed he had called for Meg, and she proceeded to walk down the drive.

'I appear to have called at an awkward time,' he drawled. 'Visiting your aunt, are you?'

Delia swung round; considering the flowers she was carrying, plus the magazines, she thought his power of deduction was pretty good. She nodded, showing she had no intention of entering into a long conversation.

'I won't keep you long,' he said.

Delia had her own thoughts on the matter. She took a deep breath. 'I don't intend to miss the bus,' she said coldly. 'It leaves in five minutes' time. I shall be in this evening, or any time tomorrow,' and she started to walk away.

She heard the car start up, and decided she wouldn't even look at him as he drove by. Her head in the air, she continued walking. It drew slowly level with her, then the car door beside her opened. 'Get in, I'll run you to the hospital,' he ordered.

Not even a 'would you' – or – 'I'd like to run you to the hospital'. The request was made to sound as if he dared her to refuse. Delia barely turned her head. 'Thank you, Mr. Sinclair, but there's no need to put yourself out. I can quite easily catch the bus.'

'The bus is not all you'll catch, if you don't get into this car pronto,' he ground out. 'I haven't all day to argue with you, but unless you want your ewe lambs treated to the spectacle of seeing their brown owl put across my knee and given a walloping, you'll do as you're told!'

Delia was so surprised she forgot to stand on her dignity, and stared at him.

'Tut, tut,' he drawled. 'It's not considered ladylike to stand with your mouth open, didn't Aunt Lucy tell you that?'

Delia's eyes blazed. 'You . . . !' she choked. 'You dare to accuse me of being unladylike! I suppose you think you're a gentleman?'

'No, ma'am,' he replied softly. 'And if you don't soon get in this car, I'll show you just how ungentlemanly I can get.'

Delia cast an agonized glance back at the house, and saw the net curtains flutter from one of the windows. There was no help for it; she clamped her lips together and got in beside him. Dane Sinclair leaned over her and slammed the door shut, an action which made her shrink back against the seat to avoid coming into contact with him.

He acknowledged the move with a raised brow. 'You're quite safe,' he said coldly. 'I like my women willing, shrinking violets bore me to tears. Tell me,' he said idly, as he started up, 'what have you got against our sex?'

Delia said nothing. He seemed to derive satisfaction by getting personal, and the best thing to do was ignore such remarks. 'What did you want to see me about?' she asked coldly.

'I'm seeing you, and talking to you,' Dane Sinclair replied grandly. 'Don't you like the conversation? Have you ever been kissed?'

To her horror Delia found herself blushing, and the knowledge that he had noted the fact made it worse. She had never met a man like this before, and felt out of her depth. As she still did not reply, he went on:

'You ought to try it some time. It's better than hearing about it secondhand. Did you know those girls look on you as a second mother? How old are you, for heaven's sake?' he demanded. 'Playing confessor to a bunch of girls, shutting yourself away like a hermit!'

Delia was stung to retort, 'I don't shut myself away!'

He gave her a quick sideways glance. 'You've not attended one of the town's social functions, have you?' he barked at her.

It occurred to Delia that he had not wasted much time in finding out about her since his arrival. 'That,' she said stiffly, 'is my affair.'

'I get it,' he drawled. 'So you have been kissed, and let down, huh? And instead of taking it on the chin, you've buried yourself, preferring to hear all about life from your young protégées.'

Delia blinked. This man was getting under her armour – yet what did he know about her? How would he feel if he had lost the only one that mattered? Yes, she had shut herself away – come thousands of miles to do just that. But she wasn't bitter, she just wanted to be left alone to pick up the pieces as best she could, and here was this cocksure man telling her what was what.

She stared out at the passing landscape. Don't listen to him, she told herself, he can't hurt you because he doesn't know.

'Don't you want a home and kids like any other woman?' he demanded. 'Because if you don't soon snap out of it they'll pass you by.'

Delia closed her eyes, she wanted to scream at him to stop. Yes, she had wanted children, and as for a home – well, she'd had that, hadn't she? And yet life had still passed her by – it passed her by when a plane crashed into a mountain. In her mind's eye she saw again the twisted wreckage they'd shown on the television. She knew she wasn't the only one deprived of someone they loved, but these thoughts did nothing to ease the heartache. She leaned her head against the car window, feeling sick.

Dane Sinclair drew up suddenly. 'Put your head down,' he commanded, and not waiting for her to comply, did it for her. A few moments later he held out a flask to her. 'Drink some of this,' he ordered.

Delia shook her head weakly. 'I'm all right now,' she said slowly.

He forced her to hold the flask. 'I said drink it,' he said quietly.

Delia's eyes came out of their glazed state, and she stared defiantly at him. 'And I said I was all right,' she said coldly, and handed it back to him.

He did not accept it. 'We go nowhere until you do as you're told,' he drawled.

She tried to outstare him but failed. She took the flask back and put it to her lips, barely tasting the liquid, then gave it back to him.

Still he would not accept it. 'This time, drink it,' he said slowly.

Delia looked at him wearily. 'Brandy isn't usually given to heat sufferers, is it?' she demanded.

His eyes narrowed. 'Is that what you're calling it?' he said, and put the flask away, to her relief. He started the car up again. 'I'd say overwork,' he said abruptly. 'Lucy's used to it – or at least, she was. You need more staff. When she's well enough, I'll have a word with her.'

Delia stared at him indignantly. He must think she hadn't heard about the new hostel. 'I don't think there'll be any need now, do you?' she said coldly. 'Eleven girls are leaving this week-end.' She deliberately spoke slowly. 'There's a new hostel – or didn't you know I'd heard about it?'

Dane Sinclair gave another of those side-glances at her, and to her fury, grinned. 'Guess I owe you an apology,' he said calmly. 'I instructed Joe Grift to write and tell you – however, his wife's been sick and I guess it went out of his head.'

Delia's eyes sparked. 'You couldn't,' she said sarcastically, 'have told me yourself, then? I'd have thought you would have enjoyed that.'

He shot her another brief glance, and Delia knew by the glint in his eye he was as mad as she was. 'There's a lot of things I'd enjoy doing right now,' he grated. 'But don't tempt me. It was a committee decision to open another hostel, and as such the information had to come through the right channels. Joe Grift is the welfare officer.'

Delia looked out at the scenery. They were almost at

the hospital. They didn't care – she thought – about taking away an old lady's income. At this rate, Aunt Lucy wouldn't even have a viable proposition to sell, just an old much outdated house. Her thoughts were racing along these lines when Dane Sinclair spoke again.

'Lost for words?' he taunted. 'Aren't you going to take me to task for suggesting it in the first place?' he said softly. 'Something on the lines of taking the bread out of an old lady's mouth?'

Her contempt showed in her eyes. 'You said it all,' she murmured. 'What do you want, confirmation? I'm only thankful I came out here,' she ground out. 'I would have hated to think of my aunt's future left to the tender administration of the town committee. We'll set up another hostel,' she said wildly. 'If that's what she wants – somewhere else, of course. – in fact, as far away as it's possible to get!'

'Feel better now?' he queried with an undertone of fury in his voice, then he braked. 'Get!' he said unceremoniously. 'You can walk the rest of the way on your own two feet. The way I feel right now you'd be safer.'

Delia got – she marched forward to the gates of the hospital, and did not look back once.

Aunt Lucy looked misguidingly frail – misguidingly, because Delia knew she had only to utter one word of sympathy and she'd jump down her throat.

Delia put the flowers on the side cabinet, and told her Mary had sent them, then gave her a peck on the cheek and sat down beside her. Aunt Lucy gave her a hard look. 'Not overdoing it, are you, girl?' she said abruptly. 'You look a bit pale to me.'

Delia smiled. 'You're not used to pale faces,' she scolded. 'I'll get a tan one of these days.' She changed the subject hastily, and went on to give her the news Mary had sent about her first grandchild. Delia wasn't sure, but she had a feeling her aunt had looked hard at her once or twice when she'd mentioned the hostel. Had she heard about the new one? she wondered, and decided to get it over with. 'There's a new hostel opening, Aunt Lucy,' she began cautiously, and watched her reaction closely.

Aunt Lucy nodded complacently, and Delia stared. 'So they've finally got around to it, have they?' she said coolly.

'You mean, you knew about it?' Delia demanded.

Her aunt nodded. 'Told me about it six months ago. Want me to run it for them. Course, it's full of new-fangled gadgets. Turned it down then, but I guess Dane will push me into it. I've got you to think about now, can't have you doing all the donkey work. Dane wants me out of the old place so he can get it modernized. Says there's enough scope for two hostels, but I've to take a back seat from now on.'

For the second time that day Delia's mouth fell open, and she stared at her aunt, then she remembered a certain comment, and closed it with a snap. Her eyes sparked – all the time he'd known, and he'd let her think . . . He'd done it deliberately! Just to get a rise out of her – and hadn't she risen to the bait! He'd even feigned fury and made her walk the last few yards to the hospital! Her hands clenched her bag – he must be laughing his head off! Oh, how she hated him!

'Weren't worrying about the new hostel, were you,

girl?' Aunt Lucy asked abruptly. 'They won't see me starve, you know.' She picked up one of the magazines Delia had brought her. 'As I said, you've no call to worry. Dane will see I'm all right, even if I refuse to take the new place on. He always has looked after me, like his father before him. One of the best.'

Delia wished she could sink through the floor. She did not anticipate the next question.

'How do you get on with him?' Aunt Lucy queried.

Delia swallowed. How do fire and water get on? she asked herself. The feeling was mutual; they couldn't stand one another. She hedged a bit. 'Haven't seen much of him,' she lied.

'You don't like him?' Aunt Lucy commented, then chuckled. 'You know, I'd an idea you two wouldn't hit it off.'

Delia said nothing.

'You'll be all right when you get to know him,' her aunt predicted confidently.

But Delia had other thoughts on the matter.

CHAPTER FIVE

LEAVING the hospital, Delia thought about Aunt Lucy's words. It looked as though she had made up her mind to accept the job of running the new hostel, and not only that – had every intention of Delia going with her. Delia pursed her lips. She would only have been too happy to comply, had it not been for Dane Sinclair. The thought of working on any project connected with him, was to say the least, abhorrent. It was utterly out of the question.

Now that her aunt's future was more or less settled, she could begin to make her own plans. As much as she disliked Dane Sinclair, she knew Aunt Lucy would be watched over; he had fully comprehended the situation, this was evident by his telling her she had to take a back seat from now on. Delia sighed; she was thankful, but how did you say 'thank you' to a man who took a delight in discomfiting you? She wondered what his reaction would be to the news of her marriage and subsequent widowhood, and shuddered. No doubt some more pearls of wisdom, as usual bluntly put. Well, he wasn't going to hear about it. It only concerned Aunt Lucy and herself. She would ask her aunt to keep the matter to herself, and Delia knew she would.

That settled in her mind, Delia began to think about her future. She would move out of the township, not too far away from Aunt Lucy, near enough, perhaps, to be able to spend week-ends with her; that way she wouldn't be too upset at her decision not to accompany her to the new hostel.

She glanced at her watch as she neared the bus stop and found she had half an hour to wait, but not wishing to stand about for that length of time, decided to while the time away in a small tea shop just beyond the stop. On the way, she passed a newsagents and stopped to purchase two papers. She would go through the advertisement section; there just might be something suitable for her. Delia had no intention of becoming idle, even though she now had a little money behind her. She thought again of what her aunt had said about Dane Sinclair doing the hostel up – could her aunt afford it? It was just one of the many questions that would have to stay in abeyance for the time being.

Finding an empty table, and checking to see she had ample time before the next bus, Delia ordered some tea and opened the papers. She was fully absorbed in her perusal of the advertisement columns when a shadow fell across her.

'Looking for a suitable dwelling to turn into a hostel, Miss Dene?' drawled Dane Sinclair.

Delia took a deep breath and gazed up into his amused eyes. Without waiting to be asked, he pulled up a chair and sat down at the table, then called out to the waitress, 'Tea for two, please.'

'Haven't you anything else to do but torment me?' Delia demanded.

He raised one eyebrow at her.

Delia raced on, 'You knew very well Aunt Lucy had been offered the running of the new hostel, yet you let me think – let me think—' She was lost for words.

'Do go on,' he said softly. 'Or shall I tell you you thought what you want to think?'

The waitress then appeared with a loaded tray, and Delia watched as she placed the contents on the table, then glanced at Dane Sinclair; was he expecting someone to join him? she wondered. He stared back at her coolly, and when the waitress left, he nodded towards the teapot. 'I prefer mine without milk,' he remarked casually.

Delia gasped, then quickly rallied. 'I'm afraid I can't stay,' she said. 'I've got the bus to catch,' she glanced at her watch; it was almost time. She gathered her papers and her bag, but Dane Sinclair rose and blocked her way.

'Sit down, Miss Dene. You're taking tea with me. I'll see you get back safely.'

Delia looked up at him, then glanced out of the café window and saw the bus approaching. If only the wretched man would get out of her way! 'I can't put you to that trouble,' she said, and made as if to pass him, but he forestalled her easily. His size alone now blocked her view. 'I've the meal to help with,' she said crossly. 'You seem to forget there are twenty girls to cater for.'

He gestured towards her chair. 'All taken care of,' he said airily. 'I've made arrangements for Mary to have some help with the dinner.'

'Who,' she snapped at him, 'is running the hostel anyway?'

He grinned, and pushed her back into her chair. 'Now you don't want me to answer that, do you?' He

58

looked back at the tea table. 'I don't care for cold tea,' he remarked autocratically.

With set lips Delia poured out his tea. He handed her a plate of scones. 'Try one,' he said. 'I can recommend them – they're good.'

'I'm not hungry,' Delia replied crossly; she knew she ought to make an effort to be more sociable, but she still hadn't got over the way he had misled her earlier.

Dane took a scone and bit into it, then had another and asked for a second cup of tea. Delia silently complied. He glanced at her sitting there with a martyred expression on her face. 'I'd say you don't eat enough,' he commented idly. 'You're too thin, also nervy. You ought to try and rest more, you know.'

Delia all but gasped. He was making her out to be an hysterical female now – let alone his blunt observations on her figure! Giving him an acid-sweet smile, she said cuttingly, 'Thank you for your interest. I'm only grateful I don't have to apply to you for a reference.'

His brows lifted. 'You do,' he said calmly.

She stared at him, only just remembering to close her lips.

He nodded. 'It's usual to ask where one last worked, isn't it?'

Delia's eyes flashed. 'You're not my employer!'

'Wrong again, Miss Dene,' he grinned. 'As chairman of the town's amenities – the hostel comes under that heading, you know – I shall be the one to give you a reference, particularly if you want to go into the hostel business again.'

Delia was so angry she absentmindedly picked up a scone and bit viciously into it. Dane watched her with an amused expression. 'Try some jam with them,' he offered consolingly. 'So,' he went on, 'it might pay to be a little less belligerent, mightn't it?'

Delia put the scone down. 'I'm not employed,' she said triumphantly. 'I'm just helping my aunt out.'

Dane shrugged. 'You're working, aren't you? You'll get a pay check at the end of the month – I don't believe in accepting free labour.'

Delia wanted to scream. The hostel then did not belong to her aunt, it belonged to him – he was telling her so.

'What sort of work are you used to?' he asked. 'I can't advise you what to take up unless I know your capabilities,' he added, fully aware that this bald statement would infuriate her.

It did, and Delia's hands clenched. Dane caught one of them and slowly unfolded it. 'A lady's hand,' he observed. 'Just beginning to show wear and tear. Whatever you did, it was not manual labour. Were you a lady of leisure?'

Delia snatched her hand away. 'No,' she grated out, 'I was not!'

'Well?' he asked.

Their eyes met briefly, and in that sudden contact Delia realized he was really interested. His blue eyes probed hers, then just as suddenly she saw the look replaced by the old teasing one. Because of that earlier look she answered his question. 'I did secretarial work,' she said quietly.

His brows rose, and he spoke in the same bantering tone that always seemed to annoy her, and Delia wondered if she had been misled earlier by his interest. 'A secretary, eh? So you didn't do the accepted thing and marry the boss?' he teased.

Delia looked away quickly, her gaze centred on the people walking past, ordinary people with ordinary lives. Mothers with their children, lovers arm in arm. How could he know how much that question had hurt? Yes – she had married the boss, against all opposition from his family, and they had had so little time to fulfil that love. Delia blinked suddenly as he barked out, 'Snap out of it!' She came back to the present with a jolt.

'So—' he said softly, 'that's what's wrong. I guessed someone had soured you. Was he married?'

It was positively the last straw. Delia gathered her things and got up quickly. 'If you don't mind,' she said coldly, 'I think I'm just in time to catch the next bus.'

As she moved away from the table, he casually remarked, 'There isn't one.'

Delia kept going. She was very near to tears and wouldn't break down in his company for anything. So there wasn't a bus. Well, it was only five miles, and she would walk it, she was fairly sure she knew the way. It would do her good to work off her feelings; at least she would have some privacy.

Fifteen minutes later, she was walking along a newly surfaced road. There was only the one main road to Sinclair. Soon she became aware of a dull ache around her heel, and stopping, she eased the strap away from the chaffed area. Her sandals, though fashionable, were not made for route marches. Moving the strap only increased the soreness, and she would have to stop every now and again to ease the strap off the blister now forming. She was limping badly by the time the car stopped. For a moment she thought it was Dane Sinclair, then when she heard the voice inquiring if she would like a lift she looked up to meet the eyes of a young man at the wheel of a flashy sports model. 'How far are you going?' he asked. Delia told him. 'Hop in,' he said. 'I'm going through there.'

Thankfully accepting the offer, she went round to the passenger seat, but before she could get in another car screamed to a halt beside them.

Dane Sinclair was absolutely furious. He caught her arm and propelled her none too gently away from the sports car to the Jaguar.

'Hey, what's on, mate? I saw her first,' protested the young man.

Still gripping Delia's arm firmly, Dane pushed her into his car before replying, 'It's my girl, mate. Want to make anything of it?'

The young man grimaced, then shrugged and got back into his car.

Delia, still recovering from the cool announcement Dane Sinclair had just made, glared at him as he got in and started up. 'Of all the—' she began, but he didn't let her finish, but guided the car off the road to a grass verge, and calmly switching off, turned to the furious Delia and caught her roughly by the shoulders, then shook her till her shoulders ached and almost reduced her to tears. As he dished out the punishment he shouted at her, 'Damn fool girl! Don't you know any better than to accept lifts from strangers? There's a shortage of women in this part of the globe. Do you want it spelt out for you?' Delia did not answer – she couldn't.

He went on in the same furious vein, 'You're not safe to be allowed out! Would have served you right if I'd left you to it. It might have done you some good, shocked you out of your self-pity and made you more human!'

He said no more, but started up the engine and drove with set lips and forbidding expression straight back to the hostel.

When they arrived Delia got out shakily. No one had ever treated her like that before. If he thought she would thank him for saving her from what he considered a fate worse than death, he was going to be disappointed! She all but ran up the hostel steps and slammed the door behind her.

Remembering what he'd said about Mary having help, Delia went straight up to her rooms. She was still trembling as she unzipped her dress and slipped it off her shoulders. Already the bluish marks were showing where he had gripped her. How dared he! She sat down shakily on the bed. 'Please, Aunt Lucy,' she whispered, 'get well soon. I can't stand much more of this.' The tears started flowing and she threw herself down and wept it out of her system.

A little while later, after Delia had bathed her eyes and tidied her hair, she heard the clutter of feet up the stairs, and someone approach her door. There was a tap and when she opened the door Meg stood there. She gave Delia a searching look and said, 'Dane says are you coming to the hoe-down tonight?'

Delia stared at her. If he hadn't a colossal nerve! Her lips set. 'Tell him I ran into a door and feel a bit frail,' she said bitterly.

Meg's eyes widened. 'Did you really? I must say you

look a bit whacked,' she said sympathetically.

Delia's expression softened. There was no point in taking it out on Meg. 'I am whacked,' she said gently. 'I intend to have an early night for once. Have a good time,' she added as she began to close the door.

Meg hesitated. 'Would you like me to stay and keep you company?' she asked.

Feeling the tears prick dangerously near the surface, Delia said hastily, 'Good gracious no! How can I rest with you chattering?'

Meg grinned and murmured, 'Point taken.'

Alone once more, Delia settled down to study the papers again. It was now absolutely imperative that she find some kind of work outside Sinclair territory.

CHAPTER SIX

A STAMPEDE down the stairs some time later told Delia the girls had gone. She was a little surprised no one had sought her help in the usual crises that seemed to occur at the last moment to the glad rags, then she smiled; Meg must have put her little foot down and made sure she was not disturbed.

There had been nothing particularly interesting in the advertisements, housekeepers needed urgently for outlying homesteads, cooks, farmhands, but not one secretarial vacancy. Delia noted several agencies asking for staff; it was a possibility that all secretarial work was handled by them, so she made a note of their telephone numbers and decided to contact them on Monday.

Sitting back in her chair, she felt her shoulders begin to ache; a hot bath, she thought, ought to ease the soreness, and it did help. Changing afterwards into jeans and a sleeveless blouse, she wandered back to the sitting-room. Settling down, she tried to interest herself in the novel that had held her attention before, but this time, however, it failed to hold her. She felt restless and wished she had not been so diligent in finishing off all the sewing requirements a few nights ago. She badly needed something to take her mind off the despondency she could feel creeping over her.

Delia then remembered the curtains in the downstairs lounge, and how there had been an ominous tearing sound as she swept them back when vacuuming that morning. She was not sure whether the curtain clips had wrenched free, or whether the curtains themselves were beyond repair.

The window was just a little below ceiling height and a step ladder would be needed for further inspection. Locating one, Delia began the inspection. Perched on the top of the ladder, she discovered it was a bit of both; the clips had become detached, but the curtains were on their last legs. Frequent washings had weakened the material, and she was just debating how she could remove the curtains on her own, as they were of a heavy damask texture, when Dane spoke.

'Frail, are you?' he said sardonically. 'Walked into a door, I hear?'

Delia was so startled she almost fell off the ladder.

'Come down from there,' he ordered. 'Do you want to break your neck?'

Delia sat surveying him from her lofty perch. She quite liked looking down on him, it made a nice change. His navy blue silk shirt and tan slacks told her he must have attended the dance, which, according to the girls, he seldom did. His red hair was brushed firmly down. From her vantage point Delia could see the fine hairs on his chest showing from his open neck, and hastily moved on with her inspection – shoes undoubtedly hand-made . . .

Dane watched her coolly. 'What do I rate?' he drawled softly.

Delia started, and had to clutch at the steps again. 'I beg your pardon?' she said coldly.

His eyes narrowed. 'Are you coming down, or have I

66

to shake you down?' he demanded.

'I've had as much shaking as I require for one day, thank you, Mr. Sinclair,' she ground out. 'I've not finished up here yet – and–' she ended lamely, not liking the look in his eye.

He moved towards the ladder. 'I warned you once,' he said, and reached out and caught her legs. With a swift movement, he whirled her off the ladder. For a brief moment he quite deliberately held her against him, then slowly he put her down.

Delia's face was flaming; she was beyond words. No man, apart from Philip, had ever held her like that. Her eyes sparked and her hands clenched.

'Go on,' he taunted softly, 'smack my face.'

And Delia did, putting all she could into it.

He lightly fingered the white mark her fingers had left. 'Feel better now?' he drawled.

She nodded. 'Much, thank you.'

'Then you won't mind if I get something off my chest as well, will you?' he murmured.

Delia braced herself for another shaking. He caught her shoulders and she winced at the touch, then he pulled her sharply towards him and kissed her hard. It was so unexpected she didn't have time to struggle; it was all over in a second.

She blinked, and moved away quickly from him when he released her. 'Why did you do that?' she asked furiously.

Dane grinned wickedly. 'Why did you slap my face?' he countermanded.

'Because I wanted to!' Delia snapped out. 'And because you asked for it!'

He nodded. 'Precisely. Any more questions?'

'None,' she answered coldly; after a statement like that there wasn't much point. She eyed him dispassionately. 'Hadn't you better get back to your guests?' she asked.

'When I'm ready,' he replied.

Delia did not like the way he stood watching her with narrowed eyes. She felt a spurt of fear; she had not quite got over that sudden kiss, and wished she knew what was going on in his mind.

To her great relief he switched his attention to the curtain rail. 'What's the trouble? Apart from old age,' he queried.

'Curtain's come away,' she answered quickly, glad they were now on a more normal subject. 'I was trying to see if I could get them down.'

He only had to climb the first three steps of the ladder and he was there. He gave a snort. 'No wonder!' he exclaimed. 'The clips are rusty. The whole place is falling apart round Lucy's ears.' He gave a sharp tug to the material, there was a rending sound, and with wide eyes Delia watched the whole rail detach itself from its fixing, bringing part of the ceiling with it.

Her eyes opened yet wider when she saw the pieces of plaster shower down on Dane Sinclair's red hair. His navy blue shirt was no longer navy blue, but a very dusty-looking article. Delia quickly clapped a hand to her mouth – if she laughed he'd kill her! She couldn't stop her thoughts, although she wished she could. Now she knew what he'd look like when he was seventy-five! With that curtain draped over his shoulders he looked like an Indian chief!

His sardonic eyes met hers. 'I dare you to as much as grin,' he said slowly.

Delia closed her eyes. If she couldn't see him perhaps she would sober up. It was no use; it gurgled up, she choked and turned hurriedly towards the door. 'I'll get a dustpan to – to—' She couldn't complete the sentence and rushed out of the room.

Collecting a brush and pan, also a clothes brush, she made her way back to the lounge. She would rather not have had to go back, but she could hardly leave him in that state. She prayed she wouldn't laugh again.

As she entered, Dane was standing in the middle of the room gazing up at the curtain rail. Delia swallowed hastily; he was absolutely plastered, she thought – what a good description this was; she wanted to giggle again.

Not meeting his eyes, she handed him the clothes brush. 'It might help,' she murmured, and as a gurgle escaped she hastily went over to the white-powdered carpet and prepared to brush up the bits trodden in.

'Leave that,' Dane commanded. 'Make yourself useful over here.'

Delia looked at him. He held out the clothes brush to her. She looked at the brush, then back at him. 'Brush me down,' he said airily. 'Not being a contortionist, I can't get to my back.'

She walked slowly back to him. He was perfectly right of course, nevertheless she didn't fancy the task at all.

Taking the brush, she patiently waited for him to turn round. Dane pointed to a patch on the top of his shoulders. 'That first,' he ordered.

69

Delia's sense of humour deserted her. He could have reached that himself, but she knew he was paying her out for laughing at him. Her lips set. 'I'm not sure I can reach,' she said quietly.

His eyes met hers. 'You can if you stand on tiptoe,' he said, and went on in a mild, slightly aggrieved tone, 'I should have thought you would have been more willing – it could have happened to you, you know.'

Swallowing her resentment, Delia gave him a wary look and reached up with the brush. 'Could you bend towards me a little?' she asked, now horribly embarrassed.

'No,' he grinned. 'You're standing too far away. You can reach if you move nearer.'

So that was his game, she thought; he was deliberately embarrassing her. Well, he was going to be disappointed! She dragged one of the stools over to where he stood and got up on it, then to his evident amusement started brushing his wide shoulders.

'Not taking any chances, eh?' he teased. 'I'm a dedicated bachelor, Miss Dene, haven't you heard?'

Delia continued brushing; the wretched stuff had got worked in. 'Yes,' she said, as if talking about the weather. 'How could I fail to, in a town this size?'

'Well, then,' he said, matching her airy tone, 'you're quite safe, so drop the panic stations act, it doesn't become your position. I expect that sort of behaviour from one of your young girls, not from you.'

Delia flushed. There he went again – referring to her as a dried-up spinster now – and all because she laughed at him! She got coolly down from the stool and placed it at his back; she didn't mind getting closer to him from that position. As she brushed, she thought about his remarks — so she wasn't acting like a house-mother, wasn't she? Let's see how he likes this approach, she thought. 'I think if you want to go back to the dance, you'll have to change your shirt, and you haven't,' she said briskly as if addressing a small boy, 'got it all out of your hair. I'll get you a hairbrush.' She walked round to face him and gave him a sweet smile. 'Then you'll be as good as new, won't you?'

He was absolutely furious. His breathing quickened, and a muscle worked at the side of his mouth.

'I'll get that hairbrush,' Delia murmured soothingly.

Dane caught her to him roughly. Delia gasped and tried to free herself. 'Really, Mr. Sinclair!' she scolded, feeling she knew how to handle him now; no longer would she be on the receiving end.

He held her closer. She could feel his hard chest against her. His hand came up behind her head forcing her to look at him, but she met his eyes calmly. House-mothers, she told her thudding heart, do not get panic-stricken, he had said so.

His eyes were on her lips. 'Being a bachelor, ma'am, doesn't stop me from kissing girls,' he said softly, 'specially saucy ones.'

Delia held on to her new-found dignity. 'Ah, girls, Mr. Sinclair. There you have it. I'm a little past that stage, aren't I? Now do be sensible and clean yourself up. Think of all those girls waiting for a dance with you.'

'I am,' he answered with narrowed eyes. 'I just thought I'd get a little practice in.'

Delia turned her head wildly, but she was no match

against his strength. His hand held her head firmly, the kiss was dynamite. She felt her senses reel. Sheer male dominance and a little punishment were mixed with a determination to make her capitulate, and she very nearly did. It awakened feelings she had thought she would never experience again, longings she had put out of her mind and heart. When Dane finally lifted his head, Delia found her head resting weakly against his strong shoulder. He looked down at her through hooded lids.

'So—' he said softly, 'you are human after all.'

Delia wrenched herself out of his arms. She hated him for doing that to her, for awakening her back to heartbreak just to satisfy his ego and make up for his loss of dignity. He wouldn't even apologize, she thought bitterly, and as if that wasn't enough, he hadn't been able to resist having another go at her. She turned her back on him and went over to where she had left the brush and pan. When he spoke again, she didn't even turn round from her task.

'So, having got warmed up, ma'am,' he announced airily, 'I'll join my party,' and left.

For a long while Delia did not move from her kneeling position. Her hands still clasped the brush and pan, her eyes were closed. How could she have been such a fool? Again she felt the warmth of his arms around her and a feeling she had felt once before when she arrived at the small township, that she had come home, swept over her. Had losing Philip done this to her? Could any man evoke such longings as Dane Sinclair had? Delia remembered that one weak telling gesture, and the tears slipped slowly down her cheeks. His eyes had acknowledged his victory over her weakness, he had got through the one chink of her armour.

She shook the wetness away. Would he now leave her alone? No! He would go on chipping away, more than likely even refer to what had happened that night. Delia knew her only salvation lay in keeping out of his way. It should not be too hard. He was an extremely busy man; only the evenings were the danger points. She never knew when he would take it into his head to call. Well, she just wasn't going to be available; she would find something to keep her out of the house when the chores were finished, even if it meant exploring the district on foot. Then she remembered the kitchen garden. As the interior of the house had been neglected, so had the hostel grounds. The kitchen garden had once produced all the vegetables the hostel required. Now Marrabee provided these items, hence the neglect of the hostel garden. Tomorrow, she decided, she would make a start on it.

CHAPTER SEVEN

FATE, it appeared, was on Delia's side. In the event there was no need for her to go out of her way to avoid Dane. On the one occasion he did call, Mary had invited Delia home for the evening to see her new grandchild.

Mary lived the other side of town, and before they turned off into a side road leading to her house she pointed to a large modern dwelling on the outskirts of the town. 'That's the Gazelle,' she said. 'Nice, isn't it? I don't mind telling you, I'm looking forward to going there. Should have gone a long time ago, but Lucy didn't fancy what she called the "new-fangled place". Got attached to the old place, I suppose. I am too. It would have been okay if she'd let Dane keep it up to date, but he's a busy man and she didn't like to worry him — leastways, that was her excuse, but I guess she liked things as they were. Well, she's got to leave now,' she grinned at Delia. 'Won't know myself,' she said confidentially. 'Cook, with two kitchen maids to assist me.' There was a hint of pride in her voice, Delia noted. 'And,' went on Mary, 'Lucy won't know herself either, that's a fact. No more cleaning for her, she won't see a duster, let alone use one. The place is fully staffed, she'll just give orders, like.'

Delia was amazed Mary knew so much, but then the subject must have been discussed many times between then. 'If you ask me,' Mary said as she opened her front door and ushered Delia in, 'that was the reason Lucy was so pigheaded each time they tried to get her to take on the new one. Didn't fancy herself acting the grand lady.'

It was late when Delia returned to the hostel. She had spent a delightful evening amongst Mary's lively family. Denny, Mary's seventeen-year-old nephew, had escorted Delia back to the hostel. Delia had not thought this was really necessary, but she was grateful for the thought.

The first thing that caught her eye when she walked in to the office was a cryptic note from Dane Sinclair, propped up on the ancient typewriter. The bold writing told her he was surprised she had deserted her post. Delia tore the note up in a temper – if that wasn't just typical of him! One minute chiding her for not joining in the town's social amenities, the next reminding her of her position!

It was Mary who warned Delia that Aunt Lucy would almost certainly be going straight to the Gazelle after her discharge from the hospital. 'She'll probably tell you on Saturday,' Mary said. 'If I know Dane, he'll insist on it. That way, there'll be no fear of her attempting to do some last-minute jobs before the move.'

Well, it made sense, Delia thought. She also wondered why Dane Sinclair had not told her this himself, then she remembered him calling on the Saturday and the previous evening. She supposed that was what he had wanted to see her about, only things hadn't worked according to plan. His ego, she thought bitterly, had got in the way.

The following day fate proved a useful ally once

75

more. Delia lost a filling and obtained an appointment straight away. There wasn't time to tell Mary of her whereabouts – besides, she did not anticipate being away more than half an hour, as the dental surgery was only five minutes from the hostel.

When she returned soon after eleven, she was met by an indignant Mary. Dane Sinclair had called, and, said Mary, seemed of the opinion that she had hidden Delia somewhere. Delia apologized, and told her what had happened. Mary sniffed and said she couldn't think where Delia had got to. She looked curiously at her. 'Seemed to think you was avoiding him – you're not, are you?' she asked.

'Now why should I do that?' replied Delia, feigning surprise.

'Well, he went charging about the place and took off in a fury.'

'If it was so important he'll ring,' Delia said soothingly. 'I am sorry, Mary.'

Giving another loud sniff, Mary went off muttering, 'No call to get so snatchy with me!'

The phone rang a short while afterwards. Delia had only just changed into her working clothes. 'Dane!' Mary called up to her. Delia sighed, and took her time in answering the call.

'So you're still resident, are you?' he asked belligerently.

Delia decided to adopt the same tactics as on their last meeting. It was safer by phone! 'Of course, Mr. Sinclair,' she answered soothingly. 'I'm so sorry I was out today. Was it anything important?'

She heard the indrawn breath and felt a surge of joy.

He was upset. No – he was furious!

'Depends,' he drawled, 'what you rate as important, Miss Dene. Where were you?'

Delia gasped. Did she now have to account for her movements? 'Nowhere important, Mr. Sinclair. I can assure you had I known you were dropping in I would have waited for you,' she said sweetly.

'Feel safe on the end of the line, do you?' he said softly.

She decided to ignore this. 'I shall be in tomorrow morning if you want to discuss anything with me,' she said brightly.

'If you don't drop that soothing tone,' he threatened, 'it won't be a discussion we'll be having, I can assure you.'

When Delia did not answer, he carried on, 'I rang to tell you you can come out of hiding. I shall be away on business for a month. I would have liked a word with you about Lucy, this morning, the doctor says he's discharging her in ten days' time. I've arranged for her to go straight to the Gazelle, for obvious reasons. You can pack up her personal stuff and take it over for her. Ring Marrabee for transport and help with any of the weighty stuff. Lucy's got a suite on the first floor. You too, of course, will be residing there.'

Delia gasped. 'I'll not be requiring accommodation, Mr. Sinclair,' she got in quickly. 'I'm seeking work elsewhere – in case you've forgotten.'

There was an ominous silence the other end of the line. When he spoke, he was angry again. 'I shall be away for one month, Miss Dene. Is it too much to ask you to keep an eye on your aunt during that time? I ought not to have to remind you that she still needs a certain amount of rest. As for a job, I've found you one. The hostel needs a secretary and I haven't anyone with those sort of qualifications. If you don't do it, Lucy will, and I don't want her worried. All she has to do is delegate the work. When I get back you can take off, if you're still determined to do so. Have I your word you won't leave until then?'

It was not an unreasonable demand and Delia knew it, but she still felt she had been cornered. 'Very well,' she replied quietly.

He seemed slightly gratified. 'When you get to the Gazelle contact Mrs. Purley, she's temporarily in charge until Lucy gets there. Got that?'

'Yes, Mr. Sinclair.' Delia cheered herself up with the thought of one whole month free from harassment.

'Right!' he shouted, and slammed the phone down.

Delia stood gazing at the receiver in her hand. What, she wondered, was he so het up about? Then she shrugged; he was a very unpredictable man!

Mary appeared from the kitchen. 'Well?' she said. 'What was so all-fired important he couldn't leave a message?'

Delia smiled. 'Oh, he just wanted to tell me Aunt Lucy's coming out in ten days' time and to get her stuff over to the Gazelle, also he's away for a month.'

Mary's eyebrows rose. 'Was that all? Well, he could have told me that, couldn't he?'

Delia was happy. 'I suppose he wanted it to go through the correct channels,' she said, her tongue in her cheek.

'So that's why Donna Smithson's giving a dinner

party tonight,' Mary murmured. 'Always gives one the night before he leaves and the day he returns.' She dried her damp hands on her overall. 'Reckon she'll never give up; no one's good enough for that madam, 'cept Dane. I'd laugh myself sick if he came back from one of his trips towing a wife behind him. There isn't anyone good enough for Dane either, come to that. Mind you, he's more call to be proud than Donna Smithson. His folk have always been the biggest land-owners around these parts. Donna's folk are jumped-ups. Her dad made his money in the trucking business. I call the time when he started with only one old bone-shaker to his name. He's gone now, so has her ma, but she don't like to be reminded of those days. Oh, no! Like I said, her dad makes a packet and they move to a classy area outside town, drop all their old acquaint-ances and send Donna to a posh finishing school in Sydney. No, sir, Donna ain't exactly popular around here. Tries to queen it over the wrong folk.'

What with one thing and another, Delia had to post-pone ringing the agencies. She couldn't move for a month now anyway, and there would be plenty of time to make the necessary inquiries. The time flew by; there was much to be done before Aunt Lucy was dis-charged. The necessary transport was at hand when-ever Delia requested it.

The Gazelle was all she had been told it was. After the old-world atmosphere of the hostel, it was like walk-ing into another world. Delia could understand her aunt's reservations on committing herself to the new life.

Mrs. Pursey, a small bustling, middle-aged woman,

showed her round the airy rooms with their contemporary furnishings and Delia found herself wondering whether the girls would be expected to pay more for such lavish accommodation. The size of the motel, too, somewhat startled her. It could take fifty girls without undue overcrowding. Delia had been rather sceptical about the need for a full-time secretary, but now she saw the position was fully justified.

Mrs. Pursey she found pleasant, but garrulous. Delia was relieved to hear she would not be staying on a full-time basis – 'Just helping out one or two afternoons a week, if Lucy required her too, that was.' Privately, Delia thought one or two afternoons would be ample. She could not see Aunt Lucy putting up with her constant chatter about everything and anything that caught her fancy.

A few days before the final evacuation, Delia received another letter from John. It reminded her to write back and instruct him to enclose her personal mail under cover of her aunt's name. He would wonder why, she knew, but he would comply. Later she would be able to explain the position to him. Delia longed for the time she would be done with all subterfuge and her status declared to the world at large.

Having read the letter, she stood frowning into space. John had hinted at new developments in the matter of the estate, he also told her he was taking an early vacation and would be seeing her in the very near future. Her frown deepened. What did he mean by 'new developments'? Surely he hadn't gone ahead and contested the will? She jumped when the cultured tones of a woman broke into her reverie.

'I'm not disturbing you, am I?'

Delia looked towards the voice and met two brown eyes, not very friendly ones. The girl standing there was quite a beauty. Her brown hair was elaborately set, her make-up faultless, and looked as if much time had been spent in getting the finished result. Her linen suit fitted her slim figure to perfection and was no off-the-peg bargain.

The girl continued after a quick appraisal of Delia, 'I suppose I ought to introduce myself. I'm Donna Smithson, and you must be Miss Dene,' she said, offering her hand as if she were conferring some honour on Delia.

There had been no need to introduce herself; Delia had already guessed her identity. She thrust the letter she was still holding into its envelope and putting it down on the desk accepted the proffered hand. 'How do you do?' she murmured politely, wondering why she had been honoured.

'I hear you're taking over the secretarial position at the Gazelle,' Donna said. 'I did offer my services in that capacity, you know, but Dane turned me down.' Her voice told Delia she had not liked that one bit. 'However,' she went on the same affected voice, 'I still intend to take an interest in the running of the hostel. My father was the amenities chairman, you know, before he died.' She gave Delia a quick assessing look. 'I understand you have secretarial experience,' she drawled, then went on as if it didn't matter whether Delia spoke or not, 'It's a very responsible position, Miss Dene, you do realize that, don't you? Of course I quite understand Dane appointing you, you have your aunt to watch over, have you not? But I just wanted to tell you I'm perfectly willing to take over if you feel the position is beyond your capabilities.' She broke off and idly flicked a speck of white off her sleeve.

Delia, watching her, felt slightly bemused, and wondered whether the girl was being deliberately offensive or truly helpful. She followed her gaze to something that seemed to be holding her attention and drew a deep breath. Donna's eyes were on the envelope she had put down on the desk, the name and address plainly visible. There was nothing she could do about it now, Delia thought ruefully, and was thankful she would soon be able to tell her aunt.

After a second or two Donna seemed to jerk back to the present. 'You see,' she said, affecting a sweet smile, 'I do know Dane's fixation for herding, as it were, his little flock, particularly those he thinks are strays, and I know he's quite likely to bulldoze you into the position without really caring whether it's suitable or not.' Having got that off her chest, she offered Delia her hand again and glided to the door. 'Do remember now, if you can't cope, just let me know.' With a careless wave, she left.

Delia stared at the closed door. She particularly resented being classed as a 'stray', and knew instinctively that there was no kind thought behind her words. One fact stood out a mile – Donna Smithson was quite furious at not being given the job. What Delia couldn't understand was why she should think it such a wonderful job anyway. The answer was not long in coming, and as usual Mary provided it.

When Delia idly commented on her visitor later that

day, telling Mary with a twinkle in her eye that Miss Smithson had offered to take over from her, Mary snorted, 'Course she would! Stands to reason, don't it?'

Delia's brows lifted. 'Does it?' she asked.

Giving her a look of exasperation, Mary said, 'The secretary takes orders from the boss, doesn't she? And who's the boss?'

'Aunt Lucy,' Delia replied promptly.

Mary sighed. 'If you ain't slow on the uptake,' she said sorrowfully. 'Dane — that's who's boss. Boss and chairman of the amenities committee — and the secretary works in close contact with the boss — that's why Miss-nose-in-the-air wants the job.'

Delia had her answer; as Mary had said, she was slow on the uptake! Well, Miss Donna Smithson was welcome to the job! Armed with this information, Delia was even more determined to 'take off' as Dane had put it, as soon as he returned.

Two days later Aunt Lucy was comfortably settled in at the Gazelle. That same evening, in the peace of their sitting-room, Delia told her about her marriage.

Aunt Lucy was quiet for a while afterwards, then she looked at Delia. 'Not much one can say, is there, girl? Only the Lord knows why these things happen, and we must accept His will,' she said gently.

Delia looked away; there was a sense of utter relief now that her aunt knew about Philip.

'Dane guessed there was something wrong,' Aunt Lucy said thoughtfully.

Delia roused herself back from the past. 'And he wouldn't let be,' she said bitterly. 'Seemed to think I was carrying a chip on my shoulder, but I'm not. I just want to be left to get over it in my own time.'

Her aunt sighed. 'Guess he can be a bit blunt. It's just his way, he means no harm, girl. He's a good man. Known him since he was knee-high. He would have left you alone if he'd known the truth.'

Delia shook her head decisively. 'That's not true, Aunt Lucy – and you know it! He wouldn't have been able to help himself interfering in what he would call my well-being.'

Aunt Lucy smiled. 'Well,' she conceded, 'perhaps you're right. Don't worry, I'll have a word with him when he returns. And with a few more folk, so that the position's clarified.' She looked at Delia. 'Is he the reason you're so set on leaving town?'

There was no call for deception, so Delia nodded. 'I know it sounds ridiculous,' she said wearily. 'But he really gets under my skin, he's so personal.'

To her relief, Aunt Lucy understood. 'Well, I'm glad we've got that sorted out. I was worried you didn't fancy staying with me, thought you might have been bored with the company of an old lady.'

Delia's eyes misted over and she caught hold of her aunt's hand. 'You're all I've got now,' she said quietly. 'I wasn't planning to move far away, you know.'

Aunt Lucy coughed hastily to cover her emotion, then said abruptly, 'Ain't no call then for you to leave. I'll settle Dane, don't you fret. I've not known him all these years for nothing. Once he knows, he'll respect your wishes. There's plenty of time for you to get acclimatized. Remember, girl, there's nothing time don't heal.' On these words the subject was closed.

Thinking about it afterwards, Delia wondered if her aunt was right in her assessment of Dane Sinclair's reaction to the news. She found herself fervently hoping so. The work was interesting and there was plenty of it. An office had been found for her just off the main reception hall and was fully equipped; even the type-writer was new.

Delia did not have quite so much contact with the girls as she had had before, but was still sought out to solve any personal problems. Soon, she knew, there would be many new faces; the new factory was open-ing in a few weeks' time. Delia had to admit she could be happy if she was left alone. She sighed; at the end of the week Dane Sinclair would be back. It was now up to Aunt Lucy.

The following day, the foreman of Marrabee called to see her; it was plain he wasn't sure of his welcome and stood a bit self-consciously in front of her. Delia smiled. 'I promise I won't bite,' she said mischievously.

He grinned. 'Dane told me to keep my distance,' he told a now indignant Delia, and went on hastily. 'Weren't sure like how you'd take our request,' he said. 'Thing is, our machine's broken down, and Dane's run out of brochures. Needs a couple of dozen in a hurry. He said if you'd make out a stencil we could run them off pronto.' He looked uncertainly at Delia. 'Got to be done more or less straight away, I've to put them on the evening plane.'

Delia immediately relieved his anxiety by asking, 'Have you brought an old one I can copy from?'

He let out a sigh of pure relief. 'Yes, ma'am,' he said happily, and produced it. 'That's it, nothing's changed,' he added.

Sorting out a stencil, Delia commented, 'Why don't you go and find Mary, if you talk nice enough to her I'm sure she'll find you some refreshment.'

As she typed out the stencil, Delia recalled Dane's barbed remark about the foreman keeping his distance and couldn't help smiling. 'You don't deserve this,' she told the stencil.

A day later Delia received a shock in the form of two dozen red roses and a hastily scrawled card that said 'Well done!' signed by Dane Sinclair. It was not only a shock, but an embarrassment as well. The bouquet was commented on from the kitchen to the cleaning staff. There had been a huge grin on the face of one of Dane's men when he marched into the hostel and presented it to her.

Delia's first thought was to get them out of the office and up to Aunt Lucy's rooms as soon as possible, but a thoughtful member of staff produced a vase from nowhere and insisted on arranging them for her. 'Look lovely on that cabinet,' she said.

Of course it just had to be the day Donna took it into her head to pay Delia a visit. As she chatted to Delia about nothing in particular, Delia saw her gaze rest several times on the roses, and that, Delia thought, was what she had really come for. She guessed the news had got around and Donna wanted confirmation. Really, anyone would think the wretched man was courting her! she thought dryly. 'I see you're admiring my roses,' she said quietly. 'Mr. Sinclair must have been relieved and very grateful,' and she went on slowly to explain the reason for his gift so there could be absolutely no misunderstanding on anyone's part.

'You could have asked me to do that,' Donna all but snapped out. 'I did offer, you know. You've got enough to do without taking on Dane's personal work. I shall have a word with that foreman of his, he'd no right to worry you.'

'It was hardly his fault,' Delia pointed out gently. 'He was told to contact me.'

This fact barely helped to calm the now seething Donna. 'Well, I shall have a word with Dane, then,' she said as she stood up abruptly and walked to the door. 'Don't worry, Miss Dene, I'll see nothing like this happens again.'

And on this note, she flounced out, leaving Delia wondering whether that had been a threat or a promise.

CHAPTER EIGHT

On the Friday, Delia had another unexpected visit from Donna Smithson. Wafting in on a cloud of expensive perfume, she casually requested Delia's presence at a dinner party she was giving that evening for Dane's return.

Delia's surprise was evident; after all, she barely knew Donna, and was puzzled by the invitation. Apart from the fact that she had no wish to attend the gathering, Aunt Lucy should have been the one to be invited. 'Perhaps my aunt—' she began.

'I've asked your aunt,' Donna said sweetly, 'and received a flat refusal. I thought you might deputize for her. I hate unbalanced numbers and must have another female. Do say you'll come.'

Delia had mixed feelings on the matter. She knew she ought to begin to attend a few social gatherings, the accusation that she had shut herself away, made so sweepingly by Dane Sinclair, could then no longer apply. With much misgivings, she accepted the invitation.

Getting ready to attend the dinner later that day, she reluctantly admitted to herself that she was actually looking forward to seeing Dane Sinclair again; although she had tried to push the thought of him out of her heart, he would keep intruding. She chided herself inwardly for her feelings – anyone would think she was an adolescent in the throes of first love! Nevertheless, she took extra pains with her toilet.

Her hair came out of the bun and fell in soft waves almost to her shoulders, and the blue gown she chose matched her eyes, its semi-flared skirt giving her slim boyish figure more substance, she thought, as she critically examined herself in the mirror, then nodded, satisfied with the effect. Just let him call her frustrated now!

For an extra measure she added eye-shadow and defiantly applied a deeper lipstick than the light, almost natural shade she normally wore. Standing back once more, she blinked rapidly. Heavens! Would anyone recognize her? She looked a different being! Her lips straightened, she was a different being! It was time to start again; to remould her life.

Picking up her coat and bag, Delia acknowledged one fact. She was beginning to take up the challenge of life again.

Aunt Lucy's brief approving nod gave her confidence. She had wondered whether she had overdone the transformation.

'Never did like that bun thing,' her aunt commented in her blunt way. 'You got your ma's hair, prettiest colour I ever did see. What you wanted to screw it up for beats me. Now you leave it be, do you hear? Time enough for a bun when you reach my age!' With these somewhat forthright remarks, she accompanied Delia to the door. 'And enjoy yourself,' she ordered.

There was no need for transport; the motel was only a short distance from Donna Smithson's home – and what an imposing one, Delia thought as she walked up the entrance drive a short while later. As she was shown in, Delia's nerves began to make themselves felt, her knees were quite weak as she was shown upstairs to a bedroom being used as a cloakroom, by an elderly lady who introduced herself as Donna's housekeeper.

From what Delia could see of the interior of the house, and the room she was shown into, no cost had been spared to create the desired effect of impressing visitors. She was suitably impressed.

As she left the bedroom, Delia met Mrs. Symes about to deposit her wrap, and felt a spurt of relief. Here was someone she did know, so she waited for her.

Mrs. Symes patted her iron-grey waves into place as she joined Delia a few moments later. 'How nice to see you,' she enthused with genuine pleasure. 'Donna mentioned that she would try and get you to come, but I know it's been difficult for you to get away before now. Taking over from your aunt at short notice like that couldn't have been easy – however, now that Lucy's on the mend you must join in a few more of our social gatherings.'

Together they walked down the stairs towards a room at the end of a corridor from where murmurings of voices could be heard. Even from that distance Delia could discern Dane's deep voice, and felt a tiny tug at her heart. She was grateful for Mrs. Symes's presence.

It was a small dinner party of eight, comprising Mr. and Mrs. Symes, Mr. Grift and his wife, now, it appeared, fully recovered from her illness, and a youngish-looking man Delia did not know, but who was later introduced as the schoolmaster. Donna and Dane completed the party.

When Delia and Mrs. Symes joined them, Donna had carelessly waved her arm towards the assembly. 'I believe you've all met,' she smiled, making no attempt to ascertain this fact.

Glancing at her, Delia was once more struck by her stunning looks. The gold lamé dress she wore clung to her well-moulded figure as if she had been poured into it. Not a hair out of place in that elaborate coiffure. In spite of her brave new look, Delia felt dispirited. Bachelor or no, this would be Dane Sinclair's type of woman.

As for the man himself, Delia carefully refrained from studying, apart from that first swift glance at him standing by Donna's side when she entered the room. She knew he wore a tuxedo and outshone every man present. She steeled herself for the inevitable teasing remarks from him on her attendance, and probably on her appearance too, if she knew him.

'I was telling Miss Dene, Dane, that she ought to come to more of our functions,' Mrs. Symes remarked.

Delia flushed slightly and looked towards Dane. Now she was for it, no doubt a few more words of wisdom, she thought. She was totally unprepared for the drawled, almost insolent reply.

'Really? That's entirely up to Miss Dene, of course,' Dane said coldly, and turned towards Donna, embarking upon an entirely different subject of conversation.

Delia's flush deepened. Mrs. Symes, after one surprised moment, hastily started to ask after her aunt's health, and Delia answered automatically. She had received a setdown in no uncertain manner by the autocratic Dane Sinclair, a fact that would be whirling around town at a great speed of knots the following day, she surmised.

Her feelings were mixed. Part of her was furious, she didn't know what she had done to deserve this treatment, the other part was deeply hurt. She wished miserably she hadn't come. Accepting a sherry, she stood slightly back from an animated discussion that had arisen between the Grifts and the schoolmaster on the siting of the new school, and saw Donna float out of the room to check up on the dinner.

Half listening to the discussion, Delia stiffened when she heard the drawling voice close beside her. 'A moment, please, Miss Dene,' said Dane, and holding her arm in no gentle fashion he drew her aside from the rest of the company.

When he considered they were out of earshot, he released his hold on her. 'I gather there's been a certain amount of speculation in town over my small gesture of thanks,' he said caustically.

Delia stared at him – the roses! she thought. Now what?

He went on in that low voice that held such fury in it, 'Certain people appear to have been given a very substantial impression of the meaning behind the gift.'

Delia said nothing; she still couldn't understand why he should be so furious. His haughty glance swept over her.

'Tell me, Miss Dene, have you hopes in that direction?'

It took a second or two for Delia to grasp the meaning behind the blunt question, then as realization dawned, a dull flush spread over her cheeks.

His cynical eyes acknowledged the heightened colour, and it was all the confirmation he needed. He smiled unpleasantly. 'It appears my appreciation somewhat misfired: I do apologize, it was meant purely as a thank you, and nothing more. There are plenty of bachelors in this town, Miss Dene – you've just picked on the wrong one.'

It was as well for Delia that Donna made her re-appearance just then. 'Dinner is served,' she announced, and turning to Dane murmured possessively, 'Your arm, please, dear.'

Delia was led into the dining-room by the school-master, who made a few idle observances on nothing in particular, which was just as well, for Delia was in no state to enter into any intelligent discussion. She was shocked to the core, and not accustomed to such accusations, if indeed anyone was. To be accused, was bad enough, to be told in no uncertain manner there was nothing doing was outrageous! Who but Dane Sinclair would have made such an assumption? Her hands clenched into fists – to think she had longed to see him again! Of the dress she had worn – and the way she had taken extra pains to look her best. She swallowed; that in itself would have been enough to confirm his suspicions.

As she was seated, she glanced up towards the head of the table at Donna seated regally at its head. So that was what she had meant when she said Delia wouldn't be troubled again! Just a few words of warning in his ear, Delia thought bitterly, that was all it would take – if anything was calculated to rouse his fury a well aimed barb in that direction topped the poll!

It was an evening Delia would not forget in a hurry. She was half-way through the meal and looking forward to the conclusion of what had been a ghastly dinner date, when events proved her ordeal was far from over. Making a valiant effort to take an interest in what the schoolmaster was talking about, she saw the housekeeper enter the dining-room and go up to Donna. Delia could not hear what was said, but she saw Donna frown and glance down at her guests. 'There's a Mrs. Courtenay wanted on the phone,' she announced gaily. 'It's probably a mistake, someone dialling the wrong number.'

Delia went white and stood up. 'I'll take it,' she announced quietly, and walking to the door noted an odd silence, then everybody started talking at once. Delia, looking straight ahead, felt rather than saw the stiffened figure of Dane Sinclair standing by his chair. When she reached the door, Donna joined her, her brows raised in silent query. 'I'll show you where the phone is,' she said sweetly.

'It's in here,' said Donna, opening a door off the hall. The room was a large lounge handsomely furnished. Delia saw the telephone with its receiver off the hook. Donna spoke again. 'I expect you'll want to be private, so I'll close the door.'

Delia looked back at her in half-surprise, then picked the phone up. As she spoke, she heard the door open again abruptly, then close. 'Mrs. Courtenay here,' she said. There was silence on the other end of the line, not even a buzzing tone. She repeated her name again. 'Who is calling, please? Is that you, John?' After a second, she heard the buzzing tone. Whoever was calling must have got disconnected, so she replaced the receiver and waited for the call to come through again.

'Quite the mystery woman, aren't you?' drawled Dane Sinclair.

Delia whirled round. He was standing near the door, his face looked as if it were chipped out of marble. 'You did say "Mrs. Courtenay", didn't you?' The voice was contemptuous. 'Was that your husband, do you think? Found out where his runaway wife had hidden herself?' He went on relentlessly in the same cold, yet dangerous voice. 'If he's come to get you back, you go – do you understand? If not with him, you go anyway. I want no trouble here. We're simple folk, Mrs. Courtenay, and masquerading under an assumed name is not considered polite.' With that he flung out of the room, leaving Delia to recover from the second shock of the evening.

For a while she stood where she was. He hadn't even bothered to ask for an explanation – which, she thought furiously, she wouldn't have given anyway! As for ordering her to leave town – it would be a pleasure! She sat down weakly on a nearby chair and prayed the call would soon come through, but after several more minutes passed, she came to the conclusion that she would not be rung back.

Leaving the lounge, she walked through the hall and up to the cloakroom. She simply could not go back to the dining-room. Collecting her coat and making her way back down the stairs, she found Donna waiting for her. 'Not bad news, I hope?' Donna asked.

Delia looked at her. There was something in the way she had said that that alerted her. Why, she's almost purring, she thought.

'Will you excuse me if I don't rejoin your guests?' Delia said quietly.

Donna smiled knowingly. 'Of course not,' she

smiled, escorting Delia to the door. 'I'm sure they understand,' she added meaningly.

Delia thought about that call as she made her way slowly back to the hostel. The call had been a hoax, of this she was practically certain. Donna had played an ace and won hands down. Delia felt a kind of relief flow through her. She hadn't liked the deception, and it had been Aunt Lucy's decision that Dane Sinclair should have been the first to be told. 'Only right,' she had said. 'He won't take kindly to hearing the news from another source.' Delia grimaced; well, he had heard from 'another source', she thought wearily, but she doubted whether Aunt Lucy would have foreseen his reaction to the news.

Letting herself into their sitting-room, Delia hoped her aunt had gone to bed; she felt utterly exhausted and had no wish to go over the evening's events. Aunt Lucy, however, had not retired, she was listening to the radio, but after taking one look at Delia, she switched off abruptly and demanded sharply, 'What's happened?'

Delia sat down wearily. It was just as well to get it over with. By tomorrow it would be all over town. By the time she had finished Aunt Lucy had a definite glint in her eye.

'No call came through here for you,' she said. 'So how come whoever was calling knew where to find you? Eh? Tell me that? You said Donna Smithson saw that letter from John, didn't you? Well, don't need to look further. Did it deliberately, I'll lay odds!' she declared. 'Spiteful little besom, she's bitten off more than she can chew this time,' Aunt Lucy added ferociously. 'I'll have her eating humble pie by this time tomorrow, or my name's not Lucy Dene!'

'It doesn't matter, Aunt,' Delia said despondently. 'It would have come out anyway, after you'd told Dane.' Her eyes were bleak. 'I'm afraid you rather miscalculated there. He told me in no uncertain terms to get out of his town. He thinks I'm a runaway wife and wants no trouble – and that,' she said bitterly, 'was after accusing me of setting my cap at him.' She broke off and looked at her aunt. 'Was there any talk in town when he sent me those roses?' she asked.

Aunt Lucy was astounded, and her mouth fell open. Delia idly wondered if that was where she had got the habit from.

Recovering swiftly, her aunt answered indignantly, 'Of course not! Leastways, I'd have heard if there was. Who said there was?'

Patiently Delia went over that episode too. 'He was absolutely certain I'd deliberately misconstrued the whole thing and took great pains in pointing out that there were plenty of bachelors to choose from, and would I kindly turn my sights elsewhere.'

'He said what!' almost shouted Aunt Lucy. 'Just wait till I see him!' she added grimly.

Delia got up. 'It's not going to make any difference,' she said firmly. 'I've taken all I'm going to take from that man.' Heading for her bedroom, she called back, 'You can tell him I'm a bigamist, if you like! He'll readily believe you. Just don't tell him the truth – at least, not until I've wiped the dust of his territory off my feet.'

Delia had only just got into bed when Aunt Lucy tapped on her door. 'You asleep?' she asked as she entered.

Delia sighed and sat up. If Aunt Lucy was going to ask her to stay she was wasting her time. However, Delia was in for a surprise.

'I've been thinking, girl,' Aunt Lucy said as she sat on her bed. 'Be a good thing if you did leave. This town's no call to hold you, and I know just the place for you to go. Got a friend, name of Amy Lacy, her husband runs a farm about fifty miles from here, near enough a town of sorts if you're still keen on getting yourself a job. Course, I don't want you to go, but I can see you've been upset. What with one thing and another, you've not had much of a welcome here, have you? Well,' she went on, 'Amy will look after you, and if I know you're there I won't worry. Perhaps by and by, when things settle down again, you can pop over to see me — or I can come and see you — how's that?'

Delia was so relieved she hugged her aunt. 'You do understand,' she said mistily.

Aunt Lucy nodded sagely. 'Not such a stupid old duffer, you know,' she said, and added, 'As one of these days you'll maybe find out!'

Delia was too relieved to query this rather odd statement.

'Now,' went on Aunt Lucy, 'I'm ringing Amy tonight and fixing for you to go early tomorrow.' She paused for a moment, then said darkly, 'And we won't use Marrabee transport either. No, sir, Jim Sparks is our man, runs a taxi business. You get your sleep in now. Just leave everything to me.'

Delia's eyes were damp as she slipped into dreamland.

CHAPTER NINE

AUNT LUCY had everything fixed by the time Delia sat down to breakfast the following morning. She even assisted Delia in packing so that she was ready to leave straight after the meal.

'Jim Sparks will drop you off at Leeton,' she told Delia. 'Amy will have you picked up from there. Where you're going is our business, and Jim don't need to know. He'll be a mite curious, I know, but you take no mind.'

Half an hour later, Delia's luggage was stowed away in the rather dilapidated-looking taxi, and she took her seat beside the driver. With one final wave from Aunt Lucy, they were away.

'Nice day for it,' commented the tubby man beside Delia.

Nice day for what? wondered Delia, and suspecting it was an opening gambit, she answered non-committally, 'Very nice.'

There was a silence for another few miles. It was not a strained one; Delia sat looking out at the passing scenery, and Jim Sparks contented himself by whistling a cheerful tune. However, he hadn't given up. 'So you're moving on, then,' he commented idly.

Delia felt she had to give some explanation, if only to change the conversation. That was the trouble with a small township, they all knew Aunt Lucy, they also knew her niece had come out from England to join her.

'I haven't,' she explained carefully, 'seen much of the country, so now that Aunt Lucy is better I'm taking what you might call a touring holiday.'

He took a few minutes to digest this information, then jerked his thumb back towards the boot containing her luggage. 'You'd do better travelling without that lot,' he said dryly.

Delia could have screamed. 'Mite curious' wasn't the expression, she thought bitterly. 'Oh well,' she answered airily, 'you never know what you'll need,' and left it at that.

'Course,' he went on, as he hooted at a slow driver, 'you'll be coming back?'

Delia found her temper wearing thin. It was a leading question, her answer was short and conveyed her determination not to pursue the subject. 'Of course,' she answered coldly.

He sighed, obviously disappointed Delia was not going to be more forthcoming, and concentrated on his driving.

They pulled into Leeton just before midday. Jim Sparks had apparently received his orders in meticulous details. Turning off the main highway, and down a side street, he eventually pulled up outside the railway station. After Delia had alighted he carried her luggage to the small waiting-room, then glancing at the station clock, said, 'Lucy told me you'd be collected. Said there was no call to wait,' he ran a hand over his stubbly chin. 'Sure you'll be okay, now?'

Delia was sure. 'Thank you for bringing me, Mr. Sparks,' she said, and held out her hand. She did not insult him by offering him a tip. Aunt Lucy had warned her of this. 'I'll settle with him,' she had told Delia. 'He knows that.'

It seemed only a matter of minutes since his departure, and Mrs. Lacy's arrival. Delia watched the woman approaching her, and judged her to be around Aunt Lucy's age. Holding a deeply tanned hand out to Delia, she introduced herself. 'Amy Lacy,' she said, with only the faintest tinge of an Australian accent. 'You've made good time.'

Accepting the hand, Delia found herself looking into two twinkling blue eyes. Mrs. Lacy's brown hair, now touched by white, had been nicely set, and Delia thought it was a shame it had had to be crushed beneath the greenish khaki bush hat adopted by so many Australians working on the land. Her dress, though fashionable, looked somehow out of place on her lean wiry figure, and Delia guessed it was not her habitual wear. Sensible shoes on her feet confirmed the feeling that Mrs. Lacy was a working woman, and judging by the deeply tanned face, worked in the open. Delia tried to place her accent, but beyond the fact that it was a northern one, she had to give up.

'Got the land-rover outside,' Mrs. Lacy said, and started gathering Delia's luggage.

Delia felt a little lost. It was all very well Aunt Lucy saying Mrs. Lacy would not mind putting her up, but had she been bludgeoned into it? 'Are you sure it's convenient?' she asked quickly.

Amy Lacy smiled. 'No trouble,' she said briskly. 'In fact, a pleasure. We don't get much company, you know – leastways, not young ladies. Got three sons – always wanted a girl, but you can't pick and choose.

Jim, my husband's, satisfied, so I can't grumble.' She gave Delia a wicked grin. 'I'd take it kindly if you'd take one of them off my hands – can't seem to get them married off nohow!'

Delia took these remarks in the spirit they were given, and smiled back at her as she followed Mrs. Lacy out to the land-rover with the rest of her luggage. 'I gather it's a cult,' she remarked. 'Bachelorism, I think it's called.'

Amy Lacy gave another of those quick grins of hers. 'You can say that again! I've nothing against one in the family, but three's ridiculous! Call themselves the Three Musketeers. You know, one for all, and all for one! Only wants one to fall flat on his face and the others will follow suit. It very nearly came off with the eldest last fall – tottering on the brink he was, and the silly chit of a girl starts flirting with some other chap to make him jealous, and that was that! Kaput! He just didn't want to know after that.'

Delia, seated in the passenger seat, found herself smiling at Mrs. Lacy's impatient tug at her skirt as she climbed into the driver's seat. 'Dratted things,' she muttered. 'Only wear 'em when I have to.'

They started off, and Delia noted with some concern that they were, in fact, heading back the way she had come. After several miles, she remarked on this, and her companion smiled. 'Wanted to put Jim Sparks off the scent. That's why I stayed out of the way until he'd vamoosed. Fact is, our land borders Dane's territory.' She glanced at Delia, who was beginning to look depressed. 'Don't worry, he's not likely to bother you – Lucy told me you'd had a brush with him.'

Delia thought her aunt's way of putting her treatment at the hands of Dane Sinclair slightly underrated!

Mrs. Lacy continued, 'Dane's okay. Got a bit of a temper, and likes his own way, of course,' she mused. Suddenly she patted Delia awkwardly on the knee. 'Heard about your trouble, girl. Right sorry too. Won't say anything else on the subject, as long as you know, like.'

'Thank you, Mrs. Lacy,' Delia said quietly.

'Heck don't call me that! Makes me feel old. You call me, Amy – okay?'

Delia smiled. 'Right – Amy.'

Within half an hour they were on the farm property. Delia, catching sight of the name 'Kerry' up on a board as they turned off down a track adjacent with the main highway, asked Amy about the name.

'Kerry?' queried Amy with a frown, then grinned. 'Land sakes! I keep forgetting you don't know the territory – that's the farm's name. Last owner was called Kerry and we never changed it. Didn't see much point, it's been called that for donkey's years. Nobody would know which place you were talking about if we changed it.' She gave Delia a quick smile. 'Course, with Lucy ill, you haven't had much chance to have a look round. Well, things are going to be a mite different from now on. Lucy wants you to enjoy yourself. Like dancing?' she shot out at Delia.

Delia looked alarmed. 'I'm not much good at it,' she said hesitantly. Not wanting to hurt Amy, she was half afraid she was going to walk into the same sort of welcome Aunt Lucy had surprised her with; however,

Amy's next words put her mind at rest.

'Guess you'd like to be a bit quiet for a while like, huh?' Amy did not miss Delia's sigh of relief. 'Yes — well, that's how I thought it might be. You take your time to settle in. Next Saturday there's a hop at the local township, be a good way to meet the folks around here. I help with the catering and we could always do with an extra hand.' She grinned at Delia. 'They fall on the food like a cloud of locusts and we're making sandwiches like the clappers in the back kitchen. As for the home-baked stuff, we never see that go — one minute the table's groaning with stuff, and the next time you turn round it looks as if world war two's been fought over it!'

Delia chuckled. 'Well, at least you know your efforts are appreciated!'

Amy grimaced. 'That's one way of looking at it, I suppose.' She gave Delia another of those quick glances. 'You don't have to help, you know, only if you've a mind to. Got a sort of feeling you'd be happier making yourself useful than sitting around looking decorative.'

Again Delia chuckled. 'I'm not exactly the decorative type, am I? No — you're perfectly right, I should love to help out.'

Soon the homestead came into view. It was a large sprawling chalet-style property, with a verandah running the length of the building. Various shrubs nestled up close to the homestead, the flowers, mostly bright pink and white, giving a picture-book effect. Delia drew a deep breath. 'Why, it's charming,' she smiled.

Amy looked gratified. 'Not so dusty, is it?' she said

proudly. 'Put a lot of work in the place, you know. You wouldn't recognize it if you'd seen it when we first took over.'

Delia's room was light and airy, and she noted various small touches thoughtfully arranged to make her feel welcome – a bowl of flowers, for instance, on the dressing-table, and an extra bright coverlet of pink quilted silk on the single bed. The quilt was brand new and had probably lain wrapped in tissue for years, either to be given as a present, or to be used for a special occasion. Delia's heart warmed to Amy, and she smiled as her fingers touched the lovely silk; had Amy hoped to be presenting this to that son of hers that had tottered on the brink? She remembered her light-hearted remark about Delia relieving her of one of them.

Delia's smile faded, her fingers drew away from the coverlet. She had so very nearly made a fool of herself over Dane Sinclair – Donna Smithson had done her a favour, did she but know it. Delia could still hear that drawling voice asking if she had hopes in that direction. Her hand clenched as she recalled the way Dane had studied her in that cold haughty way of his – certain that the extra attention she had paid to her appearance was all for his benefit. Her eyes closed. If she were honest, she would have to admit it. It had been for his benefit – without realizing how or why, she had nursed hopes in that direction, because of the way he had kissed her.

With an impatient movement she blinked the mistiness away from her eyes. She thanked providence she had had somewhere to go. The lesson had been necessary, she thought bitterly; she had so little experience, she would rather he thought her a scheming hussy than the simpleton she really was.

Changing into a light cotton frock after a shower, she had just finished brushing her hair when Amy joined her. 'Think you'll be okay here?' Amy asked hopefully.

Delia caught her hand impulsively. 'I'm sure I will, Amy,' she looked towards the flowers. 'Thank you for those,' she said quietly.

Amy grinned. 'Makes all the difference, don't it? We women have to keep our end up, we're what you might call outnumbered! But we'll get by. Come and see the rest of the homestead, we've a couple of hours before the men get back.'

As they toured the homestead, Amy pointed out parts that had been built on to accommodate their growing family. 'That's the trouble,' she sighed, as she showed Delia a room that had been made into a games area where a billiard table held pride of place. 'They're too comfortable. No wonder I can't rid of them!'

The last call was the roomy kitchen, where Delia was introduced to a large Aboriginal woman answering to the name of Bessie. Her white teeth gleamed against her polished skin as Amy introduced her, 'Been with us since Bob, my eldest, was born.'

'He sure growed up,' Bessie commented with a wide grin.

While waiting for the men, they relaxed on the verandah in comfortable cane chairs, and Amy told Delia a little of the family history. 'I'm from Yorkshire originally,' she said. 'Always wanted to go back for a visit one day. Still might, of course, if I ever get those sons of mine off my hands.'

Delia heard that Bob, the eldest, was twenty-three, and the information gave her a tiny spurt of relief; there would be no romantic complications here, in spite of Amy's half-teasing remarks.

Thudding hoofbeats in the distance announced the coming of the men. Amy pointed beyond the wheat fields to the green pastures in the distance. 'Been out on the lower slopes,' she said.

Soon they were passing the homestead and reining in. 'Do they always use horses?' queried Delia.

Amy grinned. 'It's a bit quicker,' she said in some amusement. 'Fifteen hundred acres is a bit much for the foot brigade.'

Delia's eyebrows raised. She was impressed, for she had still not got used to the great distances of this vast country.

Amy shouted across to them as they dismounted. 'You go and clean up afore you meet our guest, boys, do you hear? And that goes for you, too, Jim Lacy!'

Glancing over to where the four of them stood busy unsaddling, Delia saw a look of conspiracy pass between them as they grinned at each other. They were all about six feet tall, and she noticed the way they pushed their wide-brimmed hats back with a flick of the thumb, with almost identical actions. She looked back at Amy, not a great deal taller than herself at five feet four. Delia found herself grinning; Amy must at times feel as if she were in the land of giants – even so, she had a shrewd guess who was boss of the outfit – and it wasn't the tallest!

Fifteen minutes later four clean, well-scrubbed men presented themselves for the introductions. All wore khaki drill trousers and various coloured check shirts, all were deeply tanned, their light brown hair streaked blond in places by the sun.

Jim Lacy, Amy's husband, took precedence in the introductions. Delia, taking his hard strong hand, met two grey eyes crinkled against the glare of the sun. Had she been asked to sum Mr. Lacy up in one word, dependable was the word she would have chosen. She decided she liked Jim Lacy.

Bob, the eldest, came next. He was ridiculously like his father, the same sideways crooked grin, with his mother's blue eyes. Ray and Arthur were next in line, and Delia noted they took after their mother in looks; they had her rounded features, as against Jim Lacy's lean ascetic ones.

Arthur was teasingly introduced as 'the baby'. Delia knew him to be in his late teens, but he wasn't a bit put out, just grinned as he shook hands with her and gave the same greeting as the others, a shy, 'Howdy?'

Now that that part was over, it was Delia's turn to feel shy. She knew they were discreetly eyeing her while the conversation moved on to more general topics.

At dinner, Amy encouraged them to talk about the day's work. Dishing up for them, she commented, 'Help Delia to feel at home – besides, I want to know what sort of a day you've had.'

Delia, listening to the general talk a little while later, noted how often the boys sought their father's confirmation or advice on priorities for the morrow.

Amy might be the boss around the homestead, but there was no doubt who was boss on the farm.

Watching, and hearing their animated discussions, Delia wondered if they realized how lucky they were. She had been an only child and had had no brother or sister to fight with, or to sympathize with, when things went wrong. No doubt these boys had fought each other when they were young, it was part of growing up, and now even she could sense their companionship. Amy had said they called themselves the Three Musketeers, and inwardly she smiled; it was indeed apt. She could well imagine the three of them taking on all comers.

That evening Aunt Lucy rang, and Delia took the call in the hall. After the initial inquiries as to how Delia was settling in, her aunt went on to give her some news that was not entirely welcome. 'Dane called,' she said carefully. Delia said nothing, but her lips straightened, and she waited, knowing there was more to come. 'I guess he'd had time to cool down a bit — wanted to speak to you.' Delia remained silent. 'You still there, girl?' queried Aunt Lucy.

'Yes,' Delia replied quietly.

'Well,' went on Aunt Lucy, 'I told him I'd give you a message. He wanted to know why he couldn't speak to you, and I told him you was unavailable,' she broke off, chuckling. 'He got all riled up again.'

'Aunt Lucy, you didn't tell him I was here, did you?' Delia interrupted pleadingly.

'I was just coming to that,' replied her aunt. 'Mind you, I was mad enough with him not to, but that boy's been good to me, girl. I'm as fond of him as I am of you. I told him you were okay – and a few other things,' she added darkly. 'He felt pretty bad about what had happened, wasn't satisfied till he knew where you was.'

'Aunt Lucy! I thought we weren't going to tell anybody – least of all, him!' Delia exclaimed.

'Now, it's all right, girl,' Aunt Lucy said soothingly. 'I gave him a pretty good talking to, and he won't worry you now. As long as you know he's apologized, things will be left as they are. All you've got to do now is enjoy yourself. Do you hear?'

'Yes,' replied Delia mechanically. It didn't help knowing Dane Sinclair felt sorry for her. But her aunt broke into her musings with, 'I'd like a word with Amy.'

Calling Amy, Delia left her to it and went to her room. Her lips twisted wryly as she thought of Aunt Lucy's confident prediction that Dane would not worry her, and she found herself devoutly hoping that this time Aunt Lucy would be right.

CHAPTER TEN

On the Monday and Tuesday of the following week, Delia found much to occupy her time. Amy took her on a tour of the homestead perimeter. Pigs were kept as a sideline, and Amy took this chore on. Delia was surprised at the number kept, and knew it must mean a lot of hard work, so she offered her help to Amy.

'Land sakes! I don't do any mucking-out!' Amy grinned, guessing Delia's thoughts. 'Bessie's nephew does all that. I just keep my eye on them and occasionally feed them when Wally has to help out on the pastures. We've a few sheep, and they'll be lambing soon – then it's a case of all hands to the plough.'

The boys had argued goodnaturedly about who would have the honour of showing Delia round the farm, while Amy and Jim exchanged grins. Delia put an end to the first day's wrangling by innocently remarking, 'The thing is, I can't ride.'

They stared at her in consternation, then there was a general shout of, 'I'll teach you!'

Delia looked helplessly at Amy and Jim. Jim coughed and remarked dryly, 'I guess that comes under my department.' He gave Delia an intent look. 'If you want to learn, that is.'

Delia thought about it, then nodded. She wanted to learn, very much. She had never had the opportunity before.

Satisfied, Jim Lacy told her that Mandy was the

mare for her to start off with.

After three days' tuition, Delia felt it was just possible she might learn to ride. Her stiffness was not quite so acute, although Amy still insisted on her soaking in a hot bath after each session. Delia found she had muscles she didn't know she possessed. Invariably, she was teased by the boys, but took it all in good part.

By the Saturday, Jim Lacy prophesied she would be fit to take her maiden trot alone and unaided to the first grazing pasture. Delia at first doubted this, but by the Thursday she knew it to be true. Jim Lacy was not a person to make idle observations on anything, as she enthusiastically remarked to Amy. 'Jim was right, Amy. I shall be able to make that trip. Honestly, I never thought it would be possible!'

Amy smiled at Delia's enthusiasm and patted her on the shoulder. 'Course you will, never known Jim wrong yet,' she commented, as she placed an apron round her waist. 'Going to make some cakes for Saturday,' she explained. 'Don't forget you're helping, too.'

Delia started. She hadn't been much help around the homestead, what with the riding lessons, and Amy insisting on her resting up in the afternoons. 'Can I do anything?' she asked quickly.

'Yes,' replied Amy solemnly, 'you can go and have a hot bath – can't have you stiffening up, can we? You're on holiday, remember?'

Knowing it was no use arguing, Delia gave in and did as she was told. After a long leisurely soak in water as hot as she could bear, she changed into trews and blouse, having adopted Amy's mode of wear and discarding dresses. She then debated whether to beard

Amy in the kitchen den and insist on making some contribution for her keep; however, on second thoughts, she decided against making an issue of it. There was a saying that too many cooks spoil the broth, and Bessie would be assisting Amy anyway, so she settled on the verandah with a book Amy had found for her on the early days of the outback.

It was half-way through the afternoon when Delia heard the sound of a motor approaching the farm from the direction of the highway. Glancing up, she frowned as she spotted the familiar blue van heading for the homestead. Her heartbeat increased; she had thought it was too good to be true, and Aunt Lucy had once again been proved wrong.

Her hands clenched as she wondered whether to dive into the homestead and make herself scarce, or whether to stand her ground. It would be Dane Sinclair, not she, who was the intruder here. With narrowed eyes she watched the progress of the van as it neared the homestead, then let out a sigh of pure relief as she recognized the driver – not, as she had feared, Dane Sinclair, but Clem, his foreman. Relaxing once more, Delia told herself she ought to have known better; she couldn't see Dane Sinclair driving the van when he owned a Jaguar.

After the van had slithered to a halt opposite her, Delia watched the tall driver climb out and lift one hand in greeting. 'Howdy?' he grinned.

Delia smiled back at him; she had no quarrel with Clem. 'Mrs. Lacy's in the kitchen, I'll find her for you,' she called.

Busy opening the back of the van, Clem answered

airily, 'Hold on a bit,' and produced a huge bunch of red roses beautifully arranged as a bouquet. Delia stared at them, feeling the flush stain her cheeks. 'With the boss of Marrabee's compliments,' he said as he handed it to her with a flourish. 'There's a card inside,' he added with a wicked grin.

Deeply embarrassed, Delia had to accept the bouquet. 'Thank you,' she murmured, grateful there were no other witnesses around, and wondered if she could somehow dump them and get rid of Clem as soon as possible. However, this was not very neighbourly; it was hot and Delia knew he ought to be offered refreshment. Amy would never forgive her if it wasn't offered. With a sinking feeling she said, 'I'd better let Mrs. Lacy know you're here. I expect you could do with a drink.'

Clem followed her into the homestead, and it was obvious he knew his way around as he made straight for the kitchen. Miserably conscious of the bouquet, Delia was forced to follow.

Amy was busy with a mixing bowl when they entered. Delia swallowed convulsively and half hiding the bouquet from full sight against her leg, muttered, 'Clem brought some flowers over.'

Amy's eyes widened as she looked from Clem to Delia, then down at the bouquet. Bessie, scooping some cake mixture into tins, started giggling. 'Land sakes! Clem, is you courting Missy Delia?'

Delia gasped and Clem went a dull pink, but grinned all the same.

'Clem is not courting me,' Delia got out. 'No one is courting me! These flowers are just a gesture of . . . of friendship ... aren't they, Clem?' she appealed to the now widely grinning man.

'If you say so, ma'am,' he answered unhelpfully.

Delia flushed and looked round at the beaming faces. 'Well, I do say so!' she said firmly, thinking how once again that wretched man had put her in an embarrassing position. It was a great pity he hadn't brought the flowers himself and seen the interpretation put on them. Her lips tightened. Well, this time she would make it quite clear to all and sundry she hadn't misunderstood the gesture.

'Well?' asked Amy, going to the sink and rinsing her hands before putting the kettle on. 'Who are the roses from?'

Of all the questions that could have been asked it was the last one Delia wanted. 'Dane Sinclair,' she answered defensively, then remembered she had not read the card; perhaps Clem had got it wrong? 'At least – I think it was Mr. Sinclair,' she added.

'Card's inside,' drawled Clem with twinkling eyes.

Delia scowled at him. A great help he was turning out to be! She was forced to find the card and read the message then and there. A much brighter pink suffused her cheeks and her eyes sparkled with temper as she read the short missive. 'Well ... of all the ...' she began, and looked back at the card. 'Expect you Monday morning,' Dane had written. 'Work's piling up. Make the most of your *one week's* holiday.' It was signed with a flourish.

Bessie's high-pitched giggle broke out again. 'That there Dane courting Missy Delia – my, my!'

Delia had had enough. 'For once and for all, Dane

Sinclair is not courting me!' she all but shouted, and flung the bouquet down on the kitchen table, then taking a deep breath she looked at Clem. 'Would you take a note back for me, Clem?'

Clem's shoulders were shaking with silent laughter, but he managed to nod. Utterly disgusted with the hilarity all around her, Delia stalked out of the kitchen in search of a pen and paper.

With a glint in her eye, she sat down in her room to write to Dane Sinclair. After a moment's thought she started the letter. 'Mrs. Lacy thanks you for your kind gift of roses. There appears to be some misunderstanding. I thought my aunt would have explained the position to you. I shall not be returning.' Reading it back, she nodded, satisfied, then added, 'I believe you will find Miss Smithson willing to take over.' She was smiling as she signed her name and addressed the envelope.

On returning to the kitchen, Delia found Clem and Amy had taken their drinks out to the verandah, and went to join them. There was still a gleam of amusement in Clem's eyes as he solemnly accepted the letter, leaving not long afterwards with a drawled, 'Guess I'd better be making tracks.'

Delia watched the van disappearing down the dirt track and out of sight with smouldering eyes. That, she told herself, was one Dane Sinclair put in his place!

In spite of her plea to Amy not to mention the visitor or the roses – now safely out of sight in two vases in Delia's room – Amy said it was too good a story not to repeat. 'Land sakes! girl. What you getting so fetched up about? Can't think of a female who wouldn't feel cock-a-hoop after receiving such a gift. They're not ordinary roses by a long chalk — and according to Clem it's not the first time he's sent you roses.'

No amount of explaining the whys or wherefores of each occasion would suffice. Amy was tickled pink. 'Most eligible bachelor in the state,' she said with twinkling eyes. 'My boys don't stand a chance!'

'He's just saying sorry for shouting at me,' said Delia, now at the end of her tether. 'Honestly, Amy, there's nothing more to it. He's really done it to please Aunt Lucy — she went for him, you know.'

Amy burst out chuckling. 'Girl, you don't know Dane, that's a fact. Never known him apologize afore, and certainly not with a bucketful of roses!'

Delia eyed her dispassionately. 'Well, I told him you were very grateful for them,' she said, and felt better as she watched Amy's smile disappear and a look of absolute amazement take its place.

'You said what?' she demanded.

It was Delia's turn to grin, and she looked Amy straight in the eyes. 'Said you were grateful,' she repeated, adding meaningly, 'In case some folk got the wrong idea.'

Amy shook her head. 'He's not going to like that,' she said slowly.

'Well, he can jolly well put up with it!' Delia answered darkly.

Later that day at the dinner table, the whole tale was recounted, to Delia's embarrassment, and the boys amusement. A caricature of a lovelorn Dane was given by Bob, and Delia, unable to preserve her air of haughty aloofness, burst out chuckling. It was no use trying to convince them they were completely off the track.

They were drinking coffee on the verandah later, when Bessie appeared and announced with a huge grin that Delia was wanted on the phone. 'He said – you get that girl pronto!' she giggled.

There was no need to ask who was calling. With heightened colour Delia noted the meaning looks pass between the family accompanied by grins, as she went to take the call.

Picking the receiver up, she said coldly, 'Yes?'

'You come back Monday – is that clear?' Dane said without preamble. 'I require at least one month's notice from you.'

'Aunt Lucy,' Delia replied patiently, determined to hold on to her temper, 'was perfectly agreeable to my leaving.'

'Your Aunt Lucy,' he ground out, 'stepped out of line. She knows as well as I do we can't replace you for at least a month. Agencies have more than they can cope with at this time of year.'

'I did suggest Miss Smithson,' Delia said sweetly, and added, 'You'll find her perfectly agreeable too.'

There was a long silence and Delia gathered he was counting to ten. 'I have other plans for Miss Smithson,' he said softly.

Delia's brows raised. 'Then I hope you'll be extremely happy,' she snapped. 'But getting back to more mundane matters, I am not, repeat not, coming back!' and she slammed the phone down.

She had not quite reached the door when the phone rang again. She looked at it and sighed; it just might be

Aunt Lucy or someone else wanting Amy or Jim Lacy. Answering it, she wished she had not bothered as the furious voice of Dane once again assailed her ears.

'You dare to hang up on me again, my girl, and I'll be right over – and if I have to make that journey, you really will get what I promised you on one other occasion – remember?' he asked silkily.

Delia sighed again; she could almost imagine the scene. 'I'm listening,' she said wearily.

'That's better,' he said curtly. 'And stay listening. We've twenty to thirty girls booking in during the next two weeks, and I've no need to tell you what that entails. Before we know what's happening Lucy will be taking on the extra work.'

Delia's lips straightened. 'Aunt Lucy knows her capabilities,' she said coldly. 'And there's enough staff to cope adequately.'

'Domestic, yes,' he interrupted, 'no office staff, though. Who do you think will tackle that now you've gone?'

Delia started to say, 'Donna . . .' but again he forestalled her.

'If you are about to say Miss Smithson, I'm warning you, you're treading on dangerous ground,' he said quietly.

Delia's eyes sparked. 'I'm so sorry,' she said through clenched teeth. 'But even if—'

Again she wasn't allowed to finish. 'Even if what?' Dane said softly. 'You're jumping to conclusions again, aren't you? It's getting to be a bad habit, Delia. I should try and correct it if I were you.'

Once more Delia was tempted to slam the phone down on him, but managed to quell the impulse.

'I sure would like to see your expression right now,' he commented dryly.

Taking a deep breath, she asked coldly, 'Is there anything more you have to say, Mr. Sinclair? My coffee's getting cold.'

'Then get Amy to make a fresh pot,' he said harshly. 'Or one of the boys. I'm sure they'll be only too happy to oblige.'

'Yes, they're all perfect gentlemen,' Delia retorted quickly.

She heard the quick intake of breath before he ground out, 'Your place is with your kinsfolk – you know Lucy misses you. While you're enjoying yourself in their company you might give her a thought now and again.'

Delia felt like screaming, but made herself answer calmly, 'It might also occur to you, Mr. Sinclair, that I would still be with her if it hadn't been for you.'

He had the grace to acknowledge this. 'You do hit below the belt, don't you? Didn't you like the roses? Okay, I stand rebuked – but you come back to work on Monday, understand? I promise to keep out of your way. I can't say fairer than that, can I?'

'I'd like that in writing!' Delia said darkly.

Dane chuckled, 'Sorry, too incriminating. I'll send transport for you Sunday afternoon,' and he hung up on her.

Delia stood looking at the now silent receiver. What had she done? After a second's thought she had to admit she had done nothing; as usual, Dane Sinclair had bulldozed his way back into her existence.

With tight lips she rejoined the Lacy family on the verandah.

'Your coffee's cold,' remarked Amy, giving her a curious look. 'I'll get Bessie to make a fresh pot.'

'Oh, please don't bother,' said Delia. 'It doesn't matter.'

'Course it matters,' said Amy firmly. 'You barely had time to drink a mouthful.'

When the fresh pot arrived, a cup was poured out for Delia. She knew they were all dying to know why she had been so long on the telephone; she also knew she would have to tell them she was going back to Aunt Lucy. 'I'll be going back on Sunday,' she said quietly, adding carefully, 'Mr. Sinclair said Aunt Lucy was missing me.' She was relieved that apart from a few more meaning looks, no one queried this.

Amy sighed. 'Well, of course she would,' she said. 'But I would have liked you to stay a little bit longer,' she added despondently.

Jim Lacy coughed. 'Well, it's not as if she's going back to the U.K., is it? I mean, what's to stop her coming over for a week-end now and again, huh?'

Amy cheered up a bit at this thought and looked anxiously at Delia. 'You'll be right welcome,' she said.

Delia's eyes misted over. 'And I should love to come,' she said, and looked gratefully at Jim. 'Besides, I haven't finished my riding lessons, have I? I've no intention of giving those up.'

Amy smiled. 'That's settled, then,' she said briskly. 'We'll make a definite date before you go back.'

During the next morning's lesson, Jim referred to

Delia's next visit. Busying himself with lengthening her stirrup, he said, 'We meant it, you know. You'll be welcome any time. I'd take it kindly if you'd keep the visits up, Amy don't get much in the way of female company and she's right taken with you.' He looked away as if embarrassed, then said awkwardly, 'Course, a young girl like you will make lots of friends, I guess, but jest you remember, we'll be pleased to see you any time.'

Delia held her hand out. 'We'll shake on that,' she said gravely. 'As you put it, I'm taken with Amy too, I'll keep my promise, Jim.'

On Saturday, Delia was taken to the local hop, and despite Amy's forecast that she would be kept pretty busy backstage, she was constantly dragged out on to the dance floor, Bob, Ray, and Arthur taking it in turns to partner her. Half-way through the evening Delia spotted Clem's tall figure at the back of the hall, and remarked on this to Bob, who was partnering her in that dance. 'It doesn't look as if Marrabee's got a dance tonight,' she commented. 'Isn't that Clem over there?'

Bob looked and nodded, then glanced round the room. 'Several of Marrabee's hands are here,' he said. 'Looks as if you're right.'

Clem sought her out for the next dance. He was a very good dancer; Delia was somewhat surprised, and apologized for her lack of skill. 'I do hope I don't tread on your feet,' she said gingerly. 'I'm not up to your standard. Are all Marrabee boys so good?'

Clem grinned down at her, 'Oh, we can give you a run for your money any day!'

From the teasing light in his eyes, Delia had a feeling

he wasn't just referring to the dancing; however, she decided not to press the point, and just smiled back at him.

To Delia's utter dismay, it was Dane Sinclair who collected her the following day shortly after lunch. When Amy called out 'Dane's arrived!' Delia stood in her room gazing at her luggage and wishing she had the courage to tell him she would make her own way back, but when Bob collected the luggage, she silently followed him out of the homestead.

Dane stood talking to Jim and Amy, Delia saw he gave nothing away in height. His casual wear, against the Lacy boys' checked shirts and drill trousers, put him miles apart from the other farmers; his blue silk shirt and tapered navy slacks would not have been out of place on a yachting cruise, Delia mused. Strangely enough, no matter what he wore he would always look as if he belonged – he was that kind of man, at home in any environment. She felt her heart jerk as she walked towards the group.

He gave her a quick appraisal before inquiring sardonically, 'Enjoyed your holiday, Delia?'

He was getting to be pretty free with the use of her first name, Delia thought scathingly, and feeling the familiar rise of colour in her cheeks, answered lightly, 'Yes, thank you. I'm sorry you had to turn out, Jim or Amy would have run me back if we'd known.'

He didn't like that, a glint in his eyes said so, but he answered airily enough, 'No sense in wasting petrol. I was coming this way.' With that, he held the boot of the car open for her luggage, then nodded curtly to her. 'Door's open,' he said.

Delia had to make her farewells with him standing by. 'I'll be over in two weeks,' she promised. 'Tell Mandy to stand by.'

The first few miles were travelled in an almost pregnant silence. Delia was extremely aware of the silent man beside her and wished he would speak, but when he did she almost jumped.

'So you are going back to them for a week-end, are you?' he said sourly. 'Who, or what, is Mandy?'

Pleased to have something to talk about that was not personal, Delia explained.

Dane shot a quick look at her. 'I'll see you get riding lessons,' he said. 'No need to go traipsing back there.'

She sat up and stared at him indignantly. 'I want to go back,' she said. 'And I promised! I don't,' she said haughtily, 'break my promises.'

His eyebrows raised at this impassioned speech.

'Which one is it?' he drawled. 'I should have thought they were a bit young for you.'

Delia went white. This time he had gone far enough! 'Stop the car,' she said coldly. 'I refuse to go another yard with you,' and wildly she tugged at the door handle.

Dane reached over and jerked her away from the door, imprisoning her with one arm clamping her to his side. 'Unless you want us to land up as fatal casualties,' he bit out, 'you'll sit tight. Now, are you going to behave yourself, or are you going to stay in this position all the way back? I can manage well enough, it's automatic gearing.'

His arm felt like a steel band round her waist and

Delia could feel his hard shoulder muscles against her head. 'Well?' he demanded.

A slightly stunned Delia said shakily, 'I'll behave. Let me go, you're hurting me!'

He laughed, but released her slowly. 'Pity,' he drawled. 'You'd have been more comfortable if you'd relaxed.'

Delia resented that remark even more than the previous one. 'So much for your promise,' she said bitterly.

He glanced at her briefly. 'What promise?' he asked, then grinned. 'Oh, that. Well, you're not at the office now, are you?'

Delia did not reply, but moved as far away from him as was possible in the roomy car. After a few more miles he glanced at her again, she was staring out at the passing landscape, her fingers nervously twisting her rings, wishing the miles away so that they would soon arrive at Aunt Lucy's.

The car slowed down and Dane pulled into a layby; Delia jerked back from her musings and stared at him. What had he stopped for? He looked back at her, an unfathomable expression in his eyes. He gently pulled her restless fingers away from the rings and looked at them. 'Lucy told me,' he said quietly; their eyes met and Delia found she could not break the hold of those very blue eyes. 'Are you going to let it ruin the rest of your life?' he asked softly.

Delia wished desperately that she could understand this man – one minute dictatorial, the next outrageously provoking, and now that look she had seen once before of genuine interest, only to be replaced, she thought wearily, by yet another audacious remark should she lower her guard. 'That is my business, Mr. Sinclair,' she said quietly.

'I'm making it mine too,' he said abruptly. 'And the name's Dane, in case you hadn't noticed.'

'You're very fond of Aunt Lucy, aren't you?' she said bitingly. 'Don't worry, it doesn't affect our personal life.'

His eyes narrowed. 'What's Lucy got to do with it?' he demanded.

Delia gave him a look of sheer exasperation. 'If you don't know, I'm sure I don't,' she said wearily.

'This,' he said meaningly, 'is between you and me.'

Delia's heart lurched. He was playing games again — or was it because she was living in his town? She said as much, adding, 'I remember you saying you didn't want any killjoys around.'

Dane's eyes were hooded. 'I said between you and me,' he said slowly. 'And meant precisely that.'

Delia closed her eyes. 'There is nothing between you and me. Not now — not ever. You're quite safe you know,' she murmured softly.

'I'm safe enough,' he said, his eyes boring into hers. 'But are you? Think about it.' Then abruptly he switched on the ignition and pulled the car back on to the road.

CHAPTER ELEVEN

AUNT LUCY was pleased to see her and in a sense Delia was glad to be back. When the week-end visits were mentioned, her aunt approved. Delia felt she looked on it as some consolation to Amy after the way her visit had been so abruptly ended. 'Might even come with you,' she had said. 'It's many a long day since Amy and me got together, what with me being tied to the hostel. Now things are different,' she gave Delia a searching look. 'You sure you don't mind, girl, coming back, I mean?'

Smiling back at her, Delia replied, 'Of course not. I take after you, remember? I'm a devil for punishment.' She looked away and carefully studied the sitting-room curtains. 'Dane said he would keep out of my way, so there's no reason why I shouldn't settle down now. Did Donna Smithson offer to help out?' she asked casually.

'Wouldn't have her in the place,' growled her aunt. 'And Dane knows it. Didn't have to tell him how I felt, he knows my feelings on the matter.'

Delia sat silent. So that was why Donna couldn't take over – that, and the fact that Dane Sinclair was probably going to marry her; she could see no other explanation for his 'other plans' remark. The thought hurt and she couldn't understand why; she didn't like either of them – in fact, they deserved each other!

What with catching up on the previous week's work, and a steady trickle of new arrivals at the Gazelle,

Delia found plenty to keep her busy. The days went by smoothly.

On the Thursday she received a note from Dane telling her if she was still keen on learning to ride, he had just the horse for her and suggested she start that Saturday morning; he was coming into town and would take her back with him. Delia frowned as she read it; it was obvious he did not expect her to refuse, but she had no intention of accepting the offer. Jim Lacy would teach her to ride, and no one else.

She wrote a short note of thanks, saying she regretted not being able to accept his kind offer, then re-read the missive. Her lips twisted wryly; as usual she had to be so careful in her dealings with him. She had not forgotten his extremely odd remarks and his terse directive that she should 'think about it'. She had most certainly thought about it. On the face of it, it seemed some kind of warning that she was in danger. From him? A tiny tug at her heartstrings told her she was not entirely immune from him.

Although Delia had not seen him for almost a week, she was still very conscious of his presence; even though Marrabee was seven miles away, the feeling that he was towering over her was a tangible one. It could, of course, be allied to the fact that this was his town – that everything centred on Marrabee and its owner. Happenings at the farm were watched with avid interest and discussed by the townsfolk. Delia heard that Dane was entertaining visitors that week, and that they were staying at Marrabee, also that they were buyers – even their nationalities were known; she also knew Donna had given a dinner party for them, in all probability getting some practice in for her future role as mistress of Marrabee, she thought sourly.

After the note had been dispatched, Delia waited for the repercussions and when none came, she felt vaguely disappointed. Each time the phone rang she answered in the certainty that it would be a furious Dane demanding to know why she had refused his offer, and perhaps another drawling comment on the Lacy boys, but by the Saturday morning it was obvious that he was not going to make any such comments.

Delia knew she ought to feel relieved that her refusal had been accepted with no comebacks, but for some reason felt piqued.

The week-end was spent pleasantly, mostly on the hostel's sunny porchway with Delia getting in some sunbathing and Aunt Lucy knitting and recalling family happenings of bygone years.

In spite of the peaceful atmosphere, Delia felt strangely restless and tried to convince herself it was because she was still not quite acclimatized, but she knew it was more than that. She wondered miserably if Dane was with Donna, and gave herself a mental shake. Why shouldn't he be with her? In her mind's eye she saw Donna again and recalled how she had looked the night of the dinner party. She sighed. There was no denying she was a very beautiful woman, as if Dane or anyone else come to that, would look at her when someone like that was not only available but extremely willing to be whisked up the aisle.

Her trend of thought was brought to a close by Aunt Lucy's hesitant, 'What was your Philip like?'

Delia looked beyond her to the distant flowering

bushes – strange, she thought, it no longer hurt as much as it had done. It was as if she had moved on to another time in life – walked off one stage and on to another. The stage was as yet bare, the actors waiting off stage to come on.

'If you'd rather not talk about it, I'll understand,' Aunt Lucy said gruffly. 'Was just curious like, don't mind an old nosy biddy.'

Delia gave her a gentle smile. 'It's all right,' she said quietly. 'Of course you're interested. I think I'd like to talk about him too.' She told her aunt how they'd met, the business Philip had run. The whirlwind rush of the courtship, and the equally rushed register office wedding. Of John, and how he had seen her through that black period in her life, ending with, 'You'll like John, Aunt Lucy. Physically, he's very like Philip, they could have been brothers instead of cousins.' She sighed. 'I've only one photograph of Philip, taken while we were on honeymoon – I pushed it away in one of the desk drawers. I'll get John to find it and send it out to us.'

That night it was a long time before Delia fell asleep. Her thoughts were not unhappy ones; she would always treasure her memories of Philip, he would have wanted her to join her aunt, so she had done the right thing, and all uncertainty was now banished. It was odd really, she mused, that for all Dane Sinclair's domineering personality, he should be the one to actually say the words 'Your place is with your kinsfolk':

She turned and pushed her pillows into a more comfortable position – there she went again, thinking of Dane! It was time she began to mix and meet more people. Look how happy she had been with the Lacys.

A warm rush of gratitude flowed through her as she thought of the coming week-end and her riding lessons. Perhaps Jim would let her do another solo on Mandy – maybe even go round the farm with the boys?

Before she fell asleep, she thought of Aunt Lucy. Somehow she must persuade her to go with her; the last time she had mentioned the visit her aunt had muttered something about liking her own bed and was not one to go gallivanting about. Delia suspected there was more to it, and remembering her aunt's earlier fears that Delia would be bored by her company, thought she had the answer. Sleepily, she told herself she would have to work on it; she had a whole week in which to do it.

On Monday evening Delia brought the subject up again. 'Do come, Aunt Lucy. I'd be much happier if you were with us.'

Her aunt looked up from her knitting, a look of surprise on her face. 'Didn't Dane ring you?' she asked.

It was Delia's turn to look surprised; she shook her head. 'No, why should he?'

'Guess he left it to me to give the invitation,' murmured Aunt Lucy. 'There's a do at Marrabee on Saturday. Racing, barbecue, the whole works – kind of send-off for those visitors he's had staying with him.'

Delia stared at her. 'You didn't say we'd go, did you?'

'Of course I accepted,' answered Aunt Lucy with raised brows, as if it were unthinkable they would refuse.

Delia's lips set; he knew very well she was going to the Lacys that week-end. Still, she mused, he hadn't invited her, had he? That was why he had rung Aunt Lucy.

'Oh, well,' Delia said airily, 'you'll have to tell me all about it afterwards,' She felt a little sorry she was going to miss it.

Aunt Lucy gave her a straight look. 'No sense in that,' she said firmly, 'seeing as how you'll be there too.'

'I can't possibly go,' began Delia, 'you know I'm going . . .'

'No sense in going to Amy's either,' interrupted her aunt. 'Seeing they'll be coming over here. If I know anything about those boys, they'll be getting some practice in right now.'

Delia was nonplussed. What about Amy and Jim? Would they be coming over too? she asked her aunt.

Judging by the second show of raised brows, this question was, to say the least, hardly necessary. 'Of course they'll come,' Aunt Lucy explained patiently. 'Like me, they remember the old days.' She looked past Delia to the panelled walls. 'I mind the time when races were held every month. My, my, things were sure lively then! Dane's dad was a great one for throwing out challenges – usually won, too. They came from miles away to take part, and they'll come again, just you see. Of course,' she mused, 'town wasn't so prosperous in those days, more folk out of work than in,' she sighed. 'Can't have everything, though. Dane had to concentrate on the business end of things, and my, he did the town proud. Yes, sir, we're on the map now well and truly.' She smiled at Delia. 'Don't worry, you'll still see Amy, like as not, they'll join up with us for the day.'

Delia couldn't help wishing Dane had picked the following week-end for his 'do'. She was going to miss her riding lessons, but consoled herself with the thought that there was plenty of time.

Excitement was high throughout the rest of the week. Girls who normally went home at the week-ends booked to stay. Delia heard that the local hotel was also booked up; as Aunt Lucy predicted, people were coming from far and wide.

According to Aunt Lucy's reveries on past occasions, it was mainly the races that attracted the crowds. Bets were placed between the competing farms and ranches. As her aunt commented with a smile, 'They'll have to dig out the silverware and have a hasty polish up — must be nigh on three years since the last meeting.'

On the day, all available transport was pulled into use. Jim Sparks did a roaring trade ferrying folk out to Marrabee. Originally, transport for Aunt Lucy and Delia had been arranged from the farm, but Amy had rung through and offered to pick them up and the offer was gladly accepted.

It was a brilliantly sunny day, and as Delia got ready she was not too sure what to wear. The barbecue would be held in the evening and the evenings could be chilly. In the end she settled for an emerald green trouser suit and sleeveless white blouse. When she joined Aunt Lucy she noticed with a smile that she had 'dressed for the occasion'. Her deep blue dress was adorned with a small but lovely cameo brooch. On her head rested a large pale blue straw hat that fitted snugly over her plaits. Seeing the hat reminded Delia that she would need hers and she dashed back to get it. A loud tooting sound declared the arrival of Amy and Jim and soon they were off.

On the way there, Amy and Aunt Lucy reminisced over past race days, with Jim chirping in every now and again, the boys were making their own way there on their mounts, and Delia settled back happily and listened to the talk, but when they were on the outskirts of the farm she began to take an interest in their surroundings.

For the first time she saw the orchards, acres and acres of them. They drove for what seemed like miles and most probably was, through avenues of fruit trees. When they came within sight of the homestead, Delia held her breath. If she thought Donna's home grand, it couldn't hold a candle to Marrabee's imposing residence. Lawns surrounded the homestead broken up by beds of gorgeous flowering shrubs.

The car did not stop at the homestead but carried on past it into yet another avenue of fruit trees. Soon they came into what looked at first like pasture land, until Delia realized it was a huge paddock. From the crowds milling around, she gathered this was where the races were to be held.

Several marquees were placed at strategic points on the vast area, and she could see certain sections cordoned off from the centre, obviously marking the race track. She thought she saw Clem's tall figure in the distance adjusting the ropes, and as the car pulled into the parking area saw someone join him. This time she was sure of the identity of the man beside him. Her heartbeats increased rapidly; there was no mistaking him, and with a vague spurt of surprise, Delia knew she would be able to pick him out of a crowd anywhere, red hair or no red hair. It was something to do with the way he held his head, the slope of his broad shoulders — even the way he walked; it was all tabled away in her brain, as if it had always been there. She blinked rapidly in an effort to dispel these disturbing thoughts.

They joined the throng of people on the field and Delia saw that the women had made a special occasion of it, gay hats and equally gay dresses, plus a general air of expectancy all round. Wagers were made between the men, and every now and again was heard, 'You're on! It's a shame to take your money!'

Bob ambled up out of the crowd and gave Delia a look of feigned indignation. 'You wouldn't be biased, by any chance, would you?' he grinned. 'I was kinda hoping you'd wear our colours.' He nodded to Aunt Lucy. 'Howdy, Lucy. That's a mighty nice hat you're wearing.'

Aunt Lucy looked gratified and smiled, then looked at Amy. 'I suppose you're not biased,' she said, adding hastily as she saw the perplexed look on Delia's face replaced by one of dawning despair, 'Not the girl's fault, Bob. I forgot to mention the colours — land sakes! It's so long since we had a race.'

'I always liked them colours myself,' grinned Amy, gazing at Delia's trouser suit.

Delia looked from Amy's pale blue dress to her aunt's pale blue hat. She didn't need to ask Marrabee's colours, and she wished she had brought a coat, or a raincoat, come to that, anything she could cover herself up with. For her, the day was ruined; it didn't matter whether they believed she hadn't known – she was wearing the wretched colours, wasn't she?

When she heard the drawling voice, Delia couldn't help wondering what she'd done to deserve such happenings. Of course Dane didn't spare her. His intense blue eyes took their time in appraising her after he had welcomed the rest of the party. 'Now I call that real friendly,' he murmured with a gleam of amusement in his eyes.

Donna, materializing out of nowhere, stood by his side. She wore a white filmy dress and an emerald green picture hat with wide white organza ribbons that floated in the breeze. Her snapping eyes told Delia what she thought of her choice of colours. 'Another fan of yours, I see,' she said sarcastically.

Delia flushed and watched Dane's smile widen. 'Er ... Clem's, actually,' she snapped.

Dane's smile slowly petered out. 'Then perhaps I'd better find you a good viewing spot for the first race,' he said a trifle grimly. 'It's the only one he's taking part in.' Delia found herself propelled away from the group and led towards the track ropes. 'So it's Clem, is it?' he said dryly when they were out of earshot.

Not liking the hard hold he had on her arm, Delia wrenched herself free, but said nothing.

Dane leaned on the ropes and gazed out over the track. 'Seems some folk don't listen to what they're told,' he drawled. 'Clem's not for you.'

Delia's heart turned over, and she studiously avoided looking at him.

'Why didn't you accept my offer of riding lessons?' he shot out at her.

'I—' she started, then faltered as her eyes met his.

'You're going to lose, you know,' he said softly. 'There's no way out.'

Managing to tear her gaze away from that intent look of his, Delia hesitantly murmured, 'I . . . I don't know what you mean. I . . . don't understand you.'

He smiled at her confusion. 'Oh, I think you do,' he said gently. 'I think you understand very well indeed.'

Reprieve came for Delia in the form of a shout for Dane's presence on the starting line. With a, 'See you later,' he made his way down the track towards a group of horses about to line up for the start of the race.

Delia went in search of Aunt Lucy. Her mind in a turmoil, she was utterly incredulous. Was it remotely possible that he—? She gazed round the crowd and spotting her aunt's hat in the distance, made her way towards her. Her thoughts were still chaotic and she would have passed Donna without seeing her had not the girl caught her arm. 'Oh, don't rush away,' she said in dulcet tones. 'I've not had a chance to speak to you since the dinner party.'

Good manners forced Delia to stand and listen. Donna could not have much of a conscience, she thought as she watched her bestow a synthetic smile on her.

'Dane told me about your tragedy,' she said glibly. 'I'm so sorry,' then carefully removing one of the ribbons that had draped across her shoulder, she went on, 'Dane is terribly sorry too, but I did tell you how it was with him, didn't I? I do hope you're not going to take offence at what I'm going to say—' she hesitated, purposely taking her time. Delia bristled, but stayed calm.

'This attention he's giving you,' Donna said carefully, 'he just doesn't understand that it might be misinterpreted. He told me he was absolutely determined to make you come out of your shell and mix more with people. He's such a friendly person, you see. When we're married, I can see I shall have to curb that tendency of his, but that's Dane,' she said airily, adding meaningly, 'It's a good job I understand his motives.'

Delia felt as if she had been given a body blow. 'You're engaged, then, are you?' she asked quietly.

Donna's brows raised. 'There's an understanding,' she said haughtily. 'This is not England, you know, we don't need a ring to declare our intentions here.'

Delia took a deep breath; not for worlds would she let this woman know how she felt. She managed a smile. 'You have nothing to fear from me, Miss Smithson,' she told her lightly, and walked away leaving Donna staring after her with tight lips.

In spite of her heartache, Delia felt proud of herself. Donna hadn't liked that one bit, but then the truth always hurt, and it was hurting Delia too. Once again, she thought bitterly, she had Donna to thank for preventing her making a fool of herself over Dane Sinclair.

Rejoining Aunt Lucy and Amy, she tried to regain her composure, to listen to the lighthearted comments around them and to cheer the Lacy boys on in their individual races, to try and keep her eyes away from the winner of most of the afternoon's events, Dane.

It was too much to hope that no one would notice her quietness, and although Delia made a special effort to appear gay, Aunt Lucy, for one, was not fooled.

'You two still warring?' she asked bluntly.

Inwardly Delia groaned – so much for her gaiety! – but she answered lightly, 'Of course not! We just agree to differ.'

Her aunt grunted, 'Well, he's been trying to catch your eye most of the afternoon, that's all. Noticed you never cheered him on, more than like.'

'Aunt Lucy!' Delia exclaimed exasperatingly. 'As if he could see who was cheering him and who wasn't!'

Aunt Lucy gave her a straight look. 'All I know is, it's a good job that horse of his knew which way they were heading, as each time he passed us his eyes weren't on no track or finishing line!' she said dryly.

So Aunt Lucy had been fooled too, thought Delia sadly. 'I expect Donna's somewhere near us, then,' she answered.

'You got a touch of the sun?' Aunt Lucy demanded.

It was easier for Delia to agree with this diagnosis than to argue the point. 'I have got a headache,' she admitted slowly.

Aunt Lucy got up from the seat provided for her with a grandstand view of proceedings. 'Well, we'll pay a trip to the refreshment tent, it'll be cooler in there.' She turned to Amy. 'Coming, Amy? We're making tracks for some refreshment.'

Amy promised to follow after that race, which was the last, and Bob was taking part. He had won the first race, and Amy had hopes of him pulling off an encore!

The barbecue was held in the homestead grounds, and a stage erected in the paddock for the presentation of prizes, which, Delia learnt with a sinking feeling, was not to be until the finale, much later that evening.

When Amy had told her there would be dancing as well, Delia thought she could see a way of leaving early. Aunt Lucy would be bound to bow out around then and she would accompany her. However, the prizegiving arrangements altered this scheme. Amy and Jim, of course, would stay and see Bob receive his trophy, and Aunt Lucy elected to stay, too.

The cups were displayed on a table beside the rostrum and as they watched them placed in position, Aunt Lucy commented, 'Dane takes after his dad, kept most of them here.'

Delia, miserably watching, wished the evening away. She thought of the dancing to come and knew Dane would ask her to dance, and couldn't see how she could refuse him. For most of the afternoon he had been fully occupied in entertaining his guests, plus running the show. Delia had caught him glancing her way several times and had quickly looked away before he could hold her attention.

Seating was found for the elder folk round the freshly lighted braziers, and Delia was grateful when night fell suddenly, leaving only a glow from the fire embers. No other lighting, it appeared, was to be provided, and she wondered how the dancing could take place and asked her aunt.

'Wait till them fires really get hot,' chuckled her aunt. 'You'll see for miles around.'

Glancing back at the stage, Delia noticed with a pang of dismay that the band had arrived and were taking up their places on the stage. She dreaded the time when they would start up, and felt extremely relieved when the Lacy boys joined them after bedding down their horses in the Marrabee stables – with any luck she wouldn't be sitting around waiting for Dane to make another 'friendly' gesture by dancing with her.

Soon the smell of roast lamb pervaded the air as the heat caught the spits on which they were turned. The band struck up and Delia's hopes were fulfilled when Bob stood smartly beside her.

Ray claimed the next dance, then Arthur. Delia caught sight of Dane dancing with Donna, but there were so many people there and the dancing space so vast, it was easy to avoid close contact. If only she could keep on avoiding him, she thought, but her luck ran out after her dance with Arthur and she returned to find Dane sitting talking to Aunt Lucy.

He stood up as she approached. 'Seems,' he drawled, 'we have to get in a queue. Don't sit down,' he warned her. 'You're not stopping.'

'I need a rest,' complained Delia a trifle breathlessly.

'Then I'll carry you round the field,' he growled, and whisked her off before she could argue.

'You might,' she said crossly, 'find you have to do just that. I really am tired.'

'In that case,' he answered smoothly, 'we'll sit this one out. Somewhere nice and peaceful. You're not going back to the Lacy boys,' he added grimly.

Delia gasped indignantly. 'Well, of all the – I thought you wanted me to mix with people!' she got out.

He gave her a sideways glinting look. 'So you mix. I've no objections to Amy and Jim Lacy, or any middle-aged couple, but bachelors are out – got that?'

Delia blinked in bewilderment. 'You're a bachelor!' she said breathlessly, finding it hard to catch her breath as he was holding her wrist and pulling her along with him. She couldn't match his long loping strides. She saw they were heading for the homestead and thought of Donna's remarks about Dane's attitude to her. 'But you're different, I suppose,' she said tartly.

Again she received that glinting look. 'Glad you realize it,' he said quietly. 'I think it's time we had a little talk and stopped running round the mulberry bush.'

By this time they had reached the homestead, and still holding her firmly, Dane marched through the house and to a large comfortably furnished room. Delia had no time to take in her surroundings as he hauled her behind him; she was still busy working out the implications of his last words. 'I'm not running,' she said vaguely. 'At least, not round a mulberry bush.' She felt it about time she got to grips with the conversation – if only he would let her stand still long enough for her to concentrate.

He thrust her down into a deep armchair and stood surveying her grimly. 'What,' he shot out at her, 'was the deep freeze treatment in aid of?'

Delia was quite unable to meet his eyes, she was totally confused. This wasn't just friendliness – had he often made dead sets like this at other girls? She hadn't been mistaken before – his attitude was purely possessive. She found herself feeling sorry for Donna. How many other girls had she to drop a gentle hint to? She looked at him coldly. 'Having a last fling, Mr. Sinclair?' she inquired icily. 'I'm afraid, as I believe you once said yourself, you've picked on the wrong person.'

He stared back at her. 'Would you mind,' he asked softly, 'explaining that last remark?'

Taking a deep breath, Delia prepared to launch her attack – it was high time someone told him a few home truths. She was about to begin by telling him how sorry she felt for Donna when there was an interruption in the form of an elderly woman who after tapping on the door walked into the room.

'Yes, Jean?' he asked irritably.

'I thought I heard you,' said the woman. 'I sent a message out to you to try and locate a Mrs. Courtenay. A phone call came through for her a while ago, and they're ringing back.'

'Look no further,' he said half-wearily, and looked at Delia. 'Delia, meet Mrs. Mac, or as we call her, Jean – my housekeeper. Jean, this is Delia Courtenay.'

The woman's pleasant countenance broke into a smile as she held out her hand to Delia. 'Well, that was quick,' she said. 'I've only just sent out a message for Dane to locate you. Your husband should be ringing back any minute now.'

Delia's eyes opened wide and she was about to correct Mrs. Mac's assumption that it had been her husband calling when Dane, with set features, ushered his housekeeper out of the room.

When she had gone, he looked at Delia. 'Widow, eh? Why did you lie? Looking for sympathy, were you? Heavens above, I feel sorry for Lucy,' he bit out. 'She really fell for it!'

The strident bell of the telephone cut across this furious tirade, but Delia just sat there. It didn't matter, she told herself, what he thought. It had been a genuine mistake on his housekeeper's part; it was natural that she should assume John was her husband, as his name was the same as hers.

Dane flung across the room and picked up the receiver, listened, then held it out to Delia with an expression of disdain on his face.

Taking the receiver Delia spoke quietly. 'John?' she asked.

'Delia? At last! You do get around, don't you? I gather you're at some kind of barn dance.'

'I suppose you might call it that,' she answered, conscious of Dane's eyes boring into her and wishing he would leave. 'Where are you speaking from? Not London, surely?'

'Sydney,' he replied jovially. 'Told you I'd be taking an early vacation. I thought I'd like to tell you the news personally. Tell me, is there a decent hotel I can put up at in Sinclair?'

Delia gave him the name of the hotel, then asked, 'Would you like me to make the reservation for you? How long can you stay?'

'I'll come up tomorrow, book me in till the end of the week. I'm staying with friends in Sydney at the moment and they'd like to meet you. They knew Philip pretty well. I'd like to take you back with me for the week-end – still, we'll talk about that when we meet. I should get in about sixish – have dinner with me.'

'Yes, of course I will,' answered Delia. 'Will seven be all right?'

'Fine,' answered John. 'Oh, by the way, I can tell you something to be going on with. Your money worries are over. You'll have to wait for the rest of the news.'

'I wasn't worried, John,' she said quietly. 'What you sent me for the house was more than enough.'

'Oh, that,' he said nonchalantly. 'That was just to be going on with. Well, I suppose I'd better let you get back to the festivities. See you tomorrow at seven.'

Delia slowly replaced the receiver, and waited wearily for Dane to continue his condemnation of her character. When no words came she glanced around, to find herself alone.

If she had felt low before, she now reached an all-time level. She pushed her shoulders back and held her head high. Somehow she must get through the rest of the evening. John's voice had awakened memories she could have done without at this particular moment in time – as for Dane Sinclair – she swallowed convulsively – what had happened was for the best. She walked out and went to find Aunt Lucy.

She got back to find the whole assembly gathered around the stage, the presentation of the prizes was about to take place. Aunt Lucy, spotting her approaching, made a space for her to stand between herself and Amy. She smiled at Delia. 'Enjoying yourself, girl?' she asked.

Delia nodded dumbly and asked for the downright lie to be forgiven. She looked up towards the stage, half afraid of seeing Dane, but he was not in evidence. Donna Smithson was, very much so; she stood behind the trophies table and it was evident that she would be presenting the prizes. As the names were called, bashful men went forward to collect their cups, and each received a handshake from Donna – and no doubt a few condescending words, Delia thought bitterly, then pulled herself up sharply. It wasn't Donna's fault that the man she was to marry had a wandering eye. She was more to be pitied than disliked.

When Dane's name was called, Delia watched him leap on to the stage and saw Donna wave vaguely towards the cups. 'Help yourself,' she laughed. 'But you're not getting away with anything,' and she threw her arms round his neck and kissed him. With a heart heavy as lead Delia saw his arms go round her as he answered that kiss. Hoots and wolf whistles broke out from the watching crowd. Dane put Donna from him and turned towards them grinning. 'Bachelor's perks,' he said loudly.

Delia didn't remember much more of that day; it all passed in a haze of sheer misery. The moment Dane had kissed Donna something she had refused to acknowledge for weeks hit her. She was in love with him – and always would be. Her love was as strong as it had been for Philip – and both were denied her.

CHAPTER TWELVE

THE next morning Delia told her aunt about John's arrival, and made the necessary reservations for him at the hotel. Aunt Lucy had said it was a pity he couldn't put up at the Gazelle, but smiled and added, 'Might be a bit embarrassing for him with all these females.'

Delia had mentioned the phone call she received while she was with Dane, but said nothing about his reaction or his accusations. There was no point, she thought wearily, in upsetting her aunt again; she would no doubt sally forth once more in her defence, and Delia wanted no more trouble.

If she had been stupid enough to fall in love with Dane, that was her own fault, and somehow she must come to terms with it. To take her mind off her misery she concentrated on John's visit and the reason behind it. She thought of his remarks about her being a rich woman, or words to that effect. It sounded as if she had inherited the estate; she didn't understand how, although in a very short while she would know.

As the time approached for her meeting with John, Delia found herself in a state of nerves. She had not slept much the previous night, and knew she would not be able to face him with the calm disposition she had hoped to have.

She knew John wanted to be certain she had done the right thing in coming to Australia. Once she thought she had; now she wasn't so sure. She picked up her hairbrush and started listlessly brushing her hair. She only knew she wanted to get away. Her thoughts roamed on. If she had inherited the estate it was possible that John would want her to go back and settle things up. She stared at her reflection in the dressing-table mirror. Yes, she would go – she wouldn't have to think twice about it. She could be away perhaps for six months. She frowned. She would have to come back eventually, she couldn't desert Aunt Lucy now. If only, she thought miserably, Donna and Dane would get the wedding over; she didn't want to be in the vicinity when that happened. She swallowed convulsively and finished dressing.

Walking past the hotel reception hall and through to the lounge, Delia could see no sign of John. She glanced towards the bar and stiffened. Dane was there, and Donna seated beside him. Why had they to be there, tonight of all nights? Was he there for the purpose of railroading her and John out of his town? He was quite capable of such an action, she thought, recalling the way he had looked at her last night.

She passed on hurriedly; as yet she had not been seen and she wanted things kept that way. She prayed that John was already in the dining-room and walked quickly towards it.

When her name was called, Delia closed her eyes. He must have just entered the lounge; she turned to meet him and for a moment in time forgot about any interested onlookers. She only saw how like Philip John was. Even his style of dress, so essentially English, the same height – the same fair hair and ascetic features. Her breath caught in her throat and a lump that threatened to choke her rose swiftly. She swallowed hastily.

John caught her hand and looked anxiously at her, then caught her other hand. 'How are you?' he asked quietly.

Delia felt her eyes mist over but managed a little tremulous smile. John took a deep breath and pulled her gently into his arms and kissed her forehead. 'Sorry, dear. It still hurts, does it?'

Against his lapel, Delia nodded dumbly, then pulled herself together. 'I'm so sorry, John,' she apologized. 'Not much of a welcome, is it?' She drew away slowly from him. 'I suppose it's because I'm a bit homesick as well,' she said, hoping he would accept her excuse.

John nodded and placed an arm around her shoulders. 'Let's eat,' he suggested. 'I must admit to feeling a little peckish,' and he led Delia into the dining-room.

They ate steak with salad on the side, but Delia had little appetite; even the delicious coffee chiffon pie failed to make any impression on her numbed palate. John kept up a light conversation during the meal and she gratefully followed his lead. He was giving her time to regain her composure, and asked how she had settled down, and about Aunt Lucy and how he was looking forward to meeting her.

When they reached the coffee stage, he began to talk of other matters. 'As I mentioned on the phone,' he said, 'you'll have no money worries from now on. I ought to have remembered the briefcase.'

Delia finished her coffee and looked at him. 'Briefcase?' she queried.

He placed his coffee cup down. 'Philip's, I mean,' he

said. 'If you remember, it was thrown clear.'

Delia did remember now – only too well. It had been sent to her days after the crash. It had still been damp in places where it had lain in the snow until recovered. With it came other memories – she closed her eyes, the room felt hot.

'Delia?' John asked quickly. 'Are you all right?'

She nodded slowly. 'It's the heat. Don't worry, John, go on.'

He eyed her worriedly. 'I'm getting you some brandy.' He looked round for a waiter and frowned when he could not see one. 'I'll get it myself,' he said.

Delia roused herself. 'Please, John, don't bother, I'll be perfectly all right in a moment or so.'

John got up. 'I insist,' he said quietly. 'I ought to have thought. I needed only to say the will had been found, but like a clot I had to bring the briefcase into it. You sit tight, I won't be a moment.'

Delia's eyes closed again; holding them open was too much bother. She felt incredibly weary, and tried to concentrate on John's last words. The will had been found – it must have been made by Philip before . . . before . . .

When she next opened her eyes someone was holding her fiercely and kissing her eyelids and face. Soft tender words reached through her awakening senses. 'It's all right, my darling, you're not fighting this on your own. I tried to keep away, but I couldn't. I don't care about anything except that you're mine, and always will be. I'm here and he's not hurting you any more, do you understand?'

A sense of wonder filled her being. Delia knew whose arms she lay in, and she knew that voice, too — sometimes mocking, often harsh, but now gentle and filled with love. For a while she lay in the haven of those arms, afraid that if she moved it would all turn out to be an illusion, and that she was perhaps dreaming.

'Dane,' she said softly, and tried to get up, but he held her closer. She stared around at her surroundings, trying to make out where she was. 'What happened?' she murmured, then remembered John — she must have fainted. 'Where's John?' she asked.

Dane's face tightened. 'Marking time in the hotel office,' he said grimly. 'Just say the word and I'll have him run out of town. You're not seeing him alone again, that's for sure!'

Delia stared at him. 'John hasn't hurt me, Dane,' she cried. 'He's been wonderful to me! Oh, dear, he must be wondering what on earth's going on.'

Dane's arms fell from her, he stood up and looked down at her with narrowed eyes. 'He's not your husband?' he asked quietly.

Delia shook her head. 'He's Philip's cousin,' she said, smiling tremulously, and was shocked by Dane's reaction, he looked as if he could kill her.

'So that's the way of it,' he said softly. 'I'm beginning to feel sorry for your poor devil of a husband. Got found out, did you? Has lover boy downstairs come to join you?' He clenched his fists and turned away from her abruptly. For a while there was silence, then he threw her a key. 'You'd better let him out, hadn't you?' he ground out. 'I'm sure you can think of a plausible excuse. Something on the lines of mistaken identity,' he said bitterly.

Delia couldn't move. She wanted to run to him, but she was transfixed; she didn't understand anything any more, she only knew she loved Dane, and he was telling her to go to John.

Dane walked to the door and held it open. 'Well, what are you waiting for? – Go!' he said harshly. 'Go and find him, you make a nice pair!'

Delia stood staring at him. Slowly the implication of his words got through to her.

'What the devil are you waiting for?' he sneered. 'Or do you think I'm a better bet? Well, lady, you can count me out. It seems I miscalculated you all along the line.'

Delia just looked at him; how she loved him! 'Idiot!' she exclaimed.

He stared back at her. 'Idiot,' she repeated slowly. 'Darling idiot – come here.' She held her arms open to him.

Dane did not move; his eyes were bleak. 'If,' he said through clenched teeth, 'you're offering sympathy, I warn you, you might get more than you bargained for. I'm not in the mood for any hand-outs.' He started to leave.

'Dane,' Delia said quietly, 'go and see John, ask him why he's here – if you don't want any hand-outs as you put it, after you've seen him, I'll understand.' She turned away and walked over to the window and stood looking out.

Time passed, but Delia was not aware of it; she still stayed by the window. Events had moved a little too fast for her, and she badly needed a breathing space.

Slowly she recapped the events of the past three months. Donna had lied, she thought; Dane was not the kind of man to pledge allegiance to one woman and play around with another. All along Delia had known this, but found it hard to believe he loved her. She thought of Aunt Lucy and realized with a start that the news would come as no surprise to her. She recalled the shocked look her aunt had given Amy when Dane kissed Donna on the stage, and her subsequent quietness the rest of the evening as if she were puzzled.

She heard the door open behind her, but did not turn round, just wondered who it was.— Dane or John. Two very strong and possessive arms soon gave her the answer. She was kissed until she had no breath left and clung weakly to him.

'I ought,' murmured Dane in between kisses, 'to shake the living daylights out of you!'

'Yes, darling,' she breathed contentedly, 'but this is much more comfortable.'

So he carried on kissing her.

The following evening Dane gave an informal dinner party for just the four of them at Marrabee. John's plan of Delia accompanying him back to Sydney for the week-end was a lost cause, for Dane refused to let her out of his sight. He magnanimously told John that he would see Delia visited Philip's friends and would himself accompany her. Delia's heart lurched; when they were married was what he meant.

There was much to be discussed, for Delia was now the owner of Philip's agricultural business that made and sold farming implements all over the world. As they sat in Dane's spacious sitting-room, these affairs were discussed over coffee.

'Philip's sister was all for selling the business,' John told Delia. 'But now, of course, she doesn't have a say in it,' he said with evident satisfaction.

'No,' Delia said hastily. 'I don't want to sell, John. Philip built that business up out of nothing, he worked so hard for its success — I couldn't just let it go to the highest bidder.' Her eyes met Dane's and she wished he wouldn't look at her in quite that way. She was glad he had chosen a chair across the room from her; at least she was able to concentrate on the proceedings.

'We keep it, then,' Dane said quietly.

Delia's love shone out of her eyes. He did understand! She glanced across at John. 'You know as much about the business, John, as Philip did. What would you have done?' she queried.

John smiled. 'Exactly the same as you. I hoped this would be your decision.' He looked at Dane. 'Philip chose his managerial staff well. They're absolutely reliable and need no close supervision. I need hardly tell you the relief that will be felt when they hear the decision.'

Soon after this the men retired to Dane's office for a business discussion.

Delia glanced at Aunt Lucy, who had had the foresight to bring her knitting with her and sat contentedly clicking and listening to the conversation. There was a quiet look of satisfaction about her. Delia had not had much chance to talk to her since the previous day's momentous happenings, apart from her initial retort of, 'About time you two made up your minds!' when told by a grinning Dane.

'Aunt Lucy?' Delia said. 'You knew all along, didn't you?'

Aunt Lucy's smile widened. 'Let's say I had a notion which way the wind was blowing,' she said airily. 'Mind you, there was a time when I couldn't figure out what he was up to.' She unravelled some wool and started another row. 'To start with, he was a mite too curious about you when he visited me in hospital, and a mite too casual in his questions.' She chuckled. 'Knew you wouldn't take too kindly to his way of putting things. I guessed the sparks would fly.' She shook her head. 'Wasn't too sure, though, until he ordered you out of town.' She looked at Delia. 'That's not like Dane,' she asserted firmly. 'As long as things are peaceful like, he believes in letting folk sort themselves out. I figured there had to be another reason why he wanted you to go, and there was only one that made sense.

'So,' she said with a note of satisfaction in her voice, 'I decided it was about time you got sorted out.' Another piece of wool was unravelled. 'I sent you to Amy,' she said with a grin, 'and made Dane promise to keep his distance – before, that was, I told him where you were.' Another chuckle broke out. 'Couldn't have figured out a better way of finding out whether I was right or not. I knew if I was, he'd hook you out of there before many days had passed – and he did!'

Delia frowned, and Aunt Lucy, seeing her puzzlement, enlightened her. 'Well known fact that Amy wants them boys off her hands,' she grinned.

'Well!' said Delia in mock indignation. 'And he said you were lonely!'

'So I was,' agreed her aunt.

'He also said,' Delia continued, 'that you would tackle the office work if I didn't come back.'

'Well now,' said Aunt Lucy slowly, 'that wasn't strictly true. We could have got someone from the agencies, they'll always oblige Dane, he's too good a customer not to oblige, but he flatly refused to let me send for anyone.'

That reminded Delia of something else she wanted to ask Dane, and later when John had taken Aunt Lucy back and they were alone, she extricated herself from his arms and asked, 'What did you mean, Dane Sinclair, by saying you had plans for Donna?'

He grinned lazily and caught her to him again. 'Were you jealous?' he asked softly. 'I admit I was hoping for that reaction.' He laughed as she struggled to release herself. 'You're hooked, ma'am, I told you there was no way out, so just calm down and listen. What I said was perfectly true. I offered her the job of running the secretarial side of the new factory seeing she was so all-fired keen on helping out. Seems she felt she wasn't up to it, though,' he grinned down at Delia. 'Satisfied?' he murmured.

A little while later, Delia stirred in his arms. 'Poor Aunt Lucy,' she murmured softly, 'you did confuse her, Dane.'

There was a trace of amusement in his voice. 'If Lucy was confused, how do you think I felt? It took me long enough to fall in. I couldn't figure out why I wanted to either shake you or kiss you each time I set eyes on you – it was safer shaking you!' He was silent for a while, then said quietly, 'There's nothing like shock treatment for bringing things out. When I heard you call yourself Courtenay it hit me like a sledgehammer between the eyes. I wanted to kill you and the man whose rings you wore. I wanted you out of my territory or I felt I wouldn't be answerable for the consequences.' He kissed the tip of her nose. 'It must be true that a man in love is not quite sane. I was so crazy over you I couldn't think straight. I guess I said some pretty terrible things, my love. You should have ripped back at me – Lucy did,' he grinned wryly. 'Guess I asked for it, but she sure read me the riot act!'

'I gathered that,' chuckled Delia. 'Still, I did appreciate those roses – at least,' she added, 'when I'd got over your dictatorial note ordering me back to work!'

His eyes held a teasing light in them. 'I guess other folk appreciated them too,' he said softly. 'Kinda served two purposes at one hit. An apology for you, and a distinct warning to the Lacy boys to lay off my girl!'

Delia gasped, then remembered the meaning looks passed between the family – so it had worked, as he had known it would – the only one in the dark had been herself! 'Why, Dane Sinclair, you—' He effectively stopped the rest of the sentence.

In every issue...

Here's what you'll find:

 a complete, full-length romantic novel...illustrated in color.

 exotic travel feature...an adventurous visit to a romantic faraway corner of the world.

 delightful recipes from around the world...to bring delectable new ideas to your table.

 reader's page...your chance to exchange news and views with other Harlequin readers.

 other features on a wide variety of interesting subjects.

Start enjoying your own copies of Harlequin magazine immediately by completing the subscription reservation form.

Not sold in stores!